AN INSECT TALE

AN INSECT TALE

ALEXANDER BARTON CÁCERES

authorHOUSE®

AuthorHouse™ UK
1663 Liberty Drive
Bloomington, IN 47403 USA
www.authorhouse.co.uk
Phone: 0800.197.4150

Published by AuthorHouse 12/06/2016

ISBN: 978-1-5246-6718-4 (sc)
ISBN: 978-1-5246-6719-1 (e)

Print information available on the last page.

This book is printed on acid-free paper.

With all my heart, I would like to dedicate
this book to my family and friends.
After all, it is they who have suffered
the most in the writing of this novel.

Index

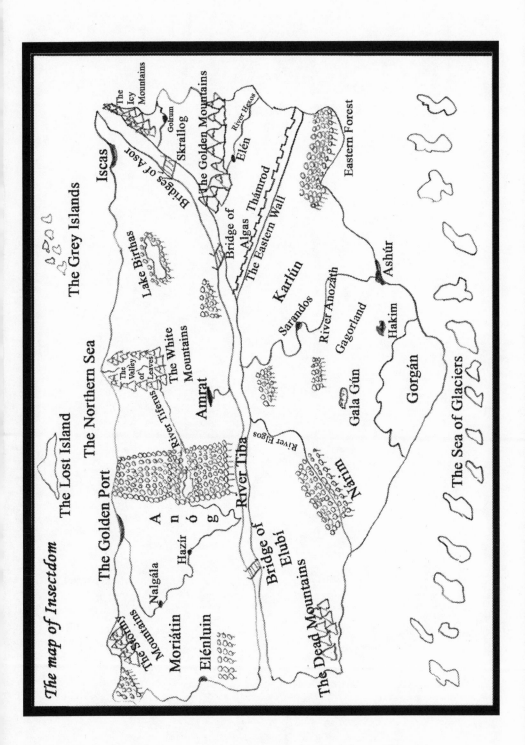

Prologue

The tale you are about to read, takes place in a world you have never heard of before, from a time long forgotten. This is the story of a world in which Insects were the dominant races that ruled the lands, the skies and the waves. It is a world of startling natural beauty and of huge contrasts. It is a land of great grass plains, of imposing mountains and of vast forests. It is a world of immense rivers, oceans, deserts and moors. It is also a world of different cultures, of great kings, of empires and of magic. On this earth the most basic and elemental passions dictate the use of power by those fortunate enough to wield it, be it vice, virtue or even vanity. Yet this will only focus on one tale: the tale of the three Kaldáre.

The world of Insectdom was large and with a long, eventful history. Kingdoms came and went, but the peoples of the world continued to live on. Change was not new to this mysterious continent, but the story that will be told has done much more to shape it than those that have come before it. This is the story of a great event long ago. The world has never been the same since then.

Yet, the origins of this tale go back even further. They go back to a time long forgotten: an age when the Insect races were only just coming into being. Many thousands of years in the misty past in the year six hundred and ten of the Insect calendar, the earliest Insect civilisations saw the arrival of a small number of mysterious visitors from a distant land across the vast expanse of the Northern Sea, known in common folklore as the Lost Island. These unusual individuals revealed themselves as Kaldáre: powerful sorcerers who had come to Insectdom as explorers, quite unsure of what they would find on the vast continent.

Much to their displeasure, they found a world which was permanently consumed by war, famine and general misery for millions of its inhabitants. So moved were the first Kaldáre by the hardships that they saw on Insectdom that they pledged to help its inhabitants and its rulers in whatever way they could. This aid could come in many forms, be it medicine, diplomacy and even as political counsel to monarchs. Every five hundred years (later on this period was increased to a millennium), three Kaldáre sailed from the Lost Island to assume the mantle of Ambassadors of their order in foreign lands, and were replaced by new sorcerers once their terms had expired.

As powerful as the Kaldáre were, even they were realistic enough to realise that it would be almost impossible to eradicate the very concept of conflict from this harsh world. War was in the blood of these races, and one cannot fight against nature itself, no matter how much the power one may possess. Nevertheless, they would do their utmost to bring about peace wherever war may be, believing that their presence as foreigners in a strange land would allow the local Insects to perceive them as politically more neutral than a native of Insectdom. With the passing of the centuries however, the Kaldáre began to perceive that they were not the only magical beings which strove to influence the creatures of this earth.

From the depths of the Underworld, a mysterious race of reptilian beasts known as the Erkúns also sought to expand their own power among the Insects on the Surface. While ruling many Insect races underground, they had also begun to exert their influence on the Insect realms long before the Kaldáre had arrived, and possessed a far more cynical, less idealistic view of the world than their foreign counterparts. Their goal was not to preserve peace, but merely to expand their own sphere of influence on the Surface, often pitting client realms against each other. Relations between the Kaldáre and the Erkúns were initially based on a mild mistrust. However with the passing of the time, the two magic wielding peoples began to view each other with outright hostility.

The poisonous contempt which both races had for each other, manifested itself in the most terrible fashion in the year four thousand one hundred and ninety eight of the Insect calendar. Repeated incidents between the Kaldáre and the Erkúns resulted in the outbreak of a terrible war which was to last over a century. For many decades vast armies of Insects clashed across hundreds of battlefields under the banners of either the Kaldáre or the Erkúns. Not a single part of the continent was spared from the scourge of conflict and all of the misery and destruction which it brought.

However, thanks to terrible strategic blunders from their enemies, the Kaldáre eventually began to gain the upper hand and in the winter of the year four thousand and three hundred finally brought about a final devastating defeat on their Underworld opponents at the Battle of Nárim. It was on the outskirts of this peaceful forest, that the Erkúns were finally broken and agreed to capitulate.

The war had proved to be devastating for the peoples of Insectdom. Almost a third of its population had been destroyed and its great cities lay in ruins, reeking of fire, ash and flesh. Determined not to let such terrible misfortune befall the world again, the victorious Kaldáre strove to establish a new world order which would ideally ensure perpetual peace.

Therefore, it was in the spring of the year four thousand and three hundred that representatives of the victors and the vanquished met on the banks of the River Tiba to discuss peace terms. It was here that the humiliated Erkúns were forced to accept punitive conditions that would later be known in folklore as the Peace of the Tiba. In order to keep the peace on Insectdom, the defeated race would never be allowed to set foot on the surface, except for one Ambassador who would serve as a liaison between the two worlds and was not to offer any form of counsel to the rulers of Insectdom.

In return, the realms on the surface would pay a monthly tribute to the Underworld in the form of precious metals, food and other goods in order to satisfy the needs of the races which lived below. Any attempt to break the terms of this treaty would be punished swiftly and severely. Despite the humiliating nature of these terms, the Erkúns were in no position to challenge them, and reluctantly agreed to comply.

Much to the surprise of the Kaldáre, this peace held together remarkably well. Eventually, the peoples of Insectdom were able to restore themselves to their former glory. The great cities of old were returned to their former grandeur, as were the lucrative trade routes which made these civilisations so wealthy. Indeed, the mightiest races of the land, the Snails, the Butterflies and the Spiders among others, enjoyed a remarkably prolonged peace by the standards of Insectdom. Admittedly, there was the occasional conflict, but it was never serious enough to bring about global instability.

As a result, these races slept peacefully knowing that their existence was protected by the Kaldáre: the great power of Insectdom. If the powers that be could rest comfortably in their cradles of power, so would the lesser beings. After all, the Erkúns of the Underworld: the sworn enemies of Insectdom were now subdued, never to return, and never willing to challenge the humiliating conditions imposed upon them. Or so they thought.

Chapter 1

Strangers in a new world

The sight of the Sun slowly rising over the horizon is something which is cherished dearly by those fortunate enough to witness such natural beauty. However, it can prove to be highly disorientating for those having to navigate at sea. As temporary as the sight of the blinding Sunlight illuminating the calm ocean may be, it is painful for those who have to endure it, depriving them of precious time to get their bearings. However, such natural obstacles were to be of no concern for those on board the ship on which this great tale begins.

The solitary vessel glided effortlessly across the misty waters of the Northern Sea. This mighty expanse of water is one of the four such seas which surrounded the imposing continent of Insectdom. The boat itself was certainly unusual for a number of reasons: a long vessel with enough space to hold almost one hundred creatures, and whose wooden hull was of an unearthly white colour, akin to that of starlight. Its sails were immense, and almost identical to the hull in colour. Yet, the sails bore an ancient symbol which few creatures on Insectdom would recognise at first glance: two, long black staffs crossed over each other, with a black

1

star above them. This was the emblem of the realm from which the occupants of this mighty vessel heralded.

If the ghostly appearance of the galley was not bizarre enough to look upon, the deck itself was even more mysterious. The ship was carried effortlessly across the water by one hundred, large white oars which worked in unison. Yet, there was no crew actually manning these mighty tools. It was almost as if an invisible magical power was controlling them from afar. Nevertheless, the ship was not completely devoid of occupants. Indeed, there were creatures on board: three of them to be precise, all sitting on the middle of the deck on white thrones of various sizes. The individuals who sat upon them were all as bizarre as the vessel itself. They were none other than Kaldáre: mighty sorcerers from the mysterious land across the Northern Sea known as the Lost Island. Few of the island's inhabitants had ever ventured across the great expanse of water to reach Insectdom, and those that did, did so very infrequently. These particular individuals were the first beings to have crossed the Northern Sea for almost one thousand years.

Sitting on the throne facing the west of the ship's destination was a Praying Mantis, one of the rarest of species. This particular individual was the first of his kind to have ventured across the sea in almost three millennia. He was very tall, very elegantly dressed, but lacked the wings his species normally has: a birth defect perhaps. His face looked youthful and innocent, but his intense eyes were the sign of an active mind. He wore a long cloak of a striking emerald colour, adorned with buttons of solid gold. In his right limb he wielded a long staff forged of some black material that was unknown to many, and at the top of this long staff, was a single jewel: an emerald at that. When the Praying Mantis spoke, he uttered his words in a deep voice which was gentle in nature, yet exuded wisdom. His name was Grizwald.

To his right sat his fellow Kaldára, Lazimóff. If the Praying Mantis was odd, in comparison with his colleague he looked positively normal. Lazimóff was a Bumble Bee, a native of the inlands of the Lost Island. He was of even larger stature to Grizwald, and whose complexion was of a black and golden colour. He wore a great red cloak, and in his left limbs wielded a great black staff, with a large ruby encrusted in its tip. Despite his size and threatening appearance, those that had met the Kaldára were often struck at how gentle he sounded when he spoke.

Last but not least, there was a third Kaldára to the right of Lazimóff: a Dragonfly by the name of Múzlak. While not as physically imposing as his Bumble Bee colleague, he would still stand out in a crowd in any Insect city of the world. His frail body was largely concealed under a cream coloured cloak, save his gigantic wings and his large eyes.

Like his fellow Kaldáre, he possessed a black coloured staff through which his power would flow, and crowned with a transparent diamond of impressive size. While Grizwald and Lazimóff exuded wisdom and gentle nature, Múzlak was the most imaginative (and at times temperamental) of the three Kaldáre. Nevertheless, he always did his utmost to restrain himself when facing a difficult situation, or indeed difficult individuals.

"The Northern Sea has been most kind to us, Lazimóff. I am Surprised that the Gods have not yet punished us with a storm," said Grizwald cheerfully to his fellow Kaldára.

"Indeed, it has been so, Grizwald. Not bad for a first voyage," replied Lazimóff.

"It is not the sea which will hold the most peril for us, I presume. It is that continent ahead of us, which will bring us most grief," said Múzlak sceptically, while looking at what lay further ahead.

"It is quite like you to bring the mood down with your pessimism, Múzlak! Nevertheless, I concede that there is logic in your words. A shambolic land mass awaits us," responded Lazimóff.

"Since when has Insectdom not been an utter shambles, my fellow Kaldára? That is the beauty of our duty: to come to the aid those less fortunate than us, and to preserve the peace that our forebears fought so hard to establish," said Grizwald.

The very mantle which the Praying Mantis spoke of was one almost as old as the world itself, and an almost sacred one at that.

"There is no need to repeat those words here, Grizwald. We are no longer standing before the Grand Council reciting our oath," said Múzlak irritably.

"There is no harm in remembering them, my dear friend," replied Grizwald sternly.

While the Kaldáre continued to converse amongst themselves, their vessel drew ever closer to its destination. In under less than one Insect hour, for the first time on their voyage, they could see with their own eyes the settlement where they would disembark.

"Behold my friends, the Golden Port!" exclaimed Lazimóff.

"Our forebears did not lie about its beauty, I see!" said Múzlak with equal enthusiasm.

Indeed, the Dragonfly was absolutely right about the pleasant appearance of the city. The Golden Port was a majestic place built many thousands of years ago by the kingdom of Moriátin: realm of the Butterflies. Despite its grand old age, it continued to be the largest and most prosperous port in the whole of Insectdom.

Barely any trade in the northern lands of the world did not pass at some stage through this great city.

As to why it was called the Golden Port, the explanation was perfectly simple. The entrance to the gigantic bay was guarded by dozens of mighty stone towers standing tall in the calm waters around the port, each decorated with a golden dome which glistened in the morning sun. Nevertheless, these majestic structures were also menacing looking, and any vessel that attempted to navigate past them without their permission, would be sent to the bottom of the sea under a hail of arrows and flaming harpoons. Indeed, no army had ever managed to successfully conquer the Golden Port neither by sea nor by land, and judging by the strength of its defences, it would come as no surprise to foreigners who visited it.

Yet, if one managed to enter the bay peacefully, then they would come across the largest gathering of ships in the known world, each disembarking their respective goods and transporting them to the temporary warehouses which stood onshore. Like every single other building in this city, every warehouse was adorned with a golden roof.

Nevertheless, the young Kaldáre would not be able to set their eyes upon the beauty of the Golden Port at a closer distance, without the permission of the guard towers. Indeed, the closer their white ship edged to the nearest fortification, the more they could sense the arming of bows and of harpoon guns within the towers around them. However, despite the apparent menace, the Kaldáre remained perfectly calm. After all, they came in peace and had no quarrel with the inhabitants of this great city.

"State your names and purpose, travellers, and you shall not be harmed," said the commanding officer of the closest tower to the Kaldáre.

5

"We come in friendship, good sir. We are Grizwald, Lazimóff and Múzlak: Kaldáre who come in name of the Grand Council of the Lost Island. We are here to relieve our predecessors Báldur, Zorza and Saldrím: mighty Kaldáre who have served their order well, but who must now part," said Grizwald confidently.

"That may be so, good sir. But I will need further proof of your identity," replied the commanding officer.

"Certainly," said Grizwald, who raised his staff and shooting a bolt of bright, green light up into the sky, startling the Butterflies guarding the towers.

"Be not afraid, my dears. We do not wish to bestow harm upon you," said Lazimóff in a reassuring tone.

"That is enough proof for me, then. You may pass freely. Your fellow Kaldáre are waiting in the harbour," said the commanding officer, still slightly startled.

"Thank you ever so much for your generosity, good sir," replied Múzlak respectfully.

With the defences lowered, the Kaldáre could now guide their vessel past the defensive towers without fear of violence. Indeed, in a very short space of time the white ship reached the mighty harbour of the Golden Port, and all three young sorcerers looked on in astonishment at the sheer size of it. It was perfectly possible for there to be over one thousand ships moored within the walls of the Golden Port, all perfectly lined up in unison.

Despite the immense size of the harbour, the Kaldáre knew perfectly well where they had to disembark: a useful advantage of having the power of foresight. Their stopping point was located at the deepest point of the port, within touching distance of city itself.

"Our stop draws near, my friends. Prepare the ship for mooring!" exclaimed Lazimóff. His instructions in turn, were obeyed by his fellow Kaldáre who each pointed their staffs downwards at the vessel. Much to the surprise of the thousands of Insects who were working in the port, the white ship docked itself, without any action on behalf of the Kaldáre who were on it.

The local Butterflies looked upon the Kaldáre with a mixture of surprise and curiosity, and the feeling was mutual. Indeed, the Kaldáre looked on in admiration at the mere physical appearance of their hosts. The Butterflies were generally tall creatures, famous for adorning their frail bodies with colourful tunics (with the exception of the city's soldiers, who wore dark green armour). This being a port city however, colourful outfits were not very common, tending to be the exception rather than the rule. Far more habitual, was the wearing of dull rudimentary clothing far more suited to the handling of goods.

Yet for their unassuming physique, the Butterflies compensated for it with their impressive wings. They were far larger than the bodies that had them and were of a stunning variety of colours. Some of them had wings as red as rubies, others as blue as the sky itself. The Elders on the Grand Council told the young Kaldáre always told their younger peers that they considered the Butterflies to be the most beautiful of all Insects in the world.

Such words now resonated very much with the three Kaldáre. However despite their legendary beauty, Butterflies also had a stereotypical reputation for displaying a thinly veiled arrogance and contempt towards Insects they deemed not as sophisticated as themselves. This in turn, put most races into this category. In the case of the Kaldáre however, this was to be an exception.

Once the ship had finished docking itself, the three young Kaldáre stepped off the vessel and on to the pier, in order to greet the welcome party which awaited them anxiously. Indeed, there were around a dozen Insects standing before them, and of a variety of races, specifically nine Butterflies, one Ladybird, one Centipede and one Cricket.

Three of the Butterflies wore civilian attire in the form of long green and white robes, while the others wore military garb. Yet, it was the non-Butterflies among the party which drew the attention of the newcomers. For these bizarre looking creatures were the very sorcerers that they had come to replace. The Ladybird was female and with a gentle, wizened face, her body concealed under a long purple cloak and wielding a long black staff, with a bright blue sapphire encrusted at the top. To her right stood the Centipede, who in comparison was rather more imposing in size, and with a sterner expression. Indeed, the tattered grey cloak which the creature wore left little to the imagination of just how big it was. It too wielded a mighty staff in its limbs, yet adorned with a diamond instead. Last but not least was the Cricket. Of a similar size to Grizwald, the ancient creature stood out more than his fellow sorcerers, thanks to the golden robes which he wore, and his large wings which protruded from behind. Like his Centipede colleague, his black staff, was adorned with a ruby.

"Grizwald, Lazimóff and Múzlak, I presume," said the Ladybird, with a gentle female voice.

"Indeed, we are. Judging by your splendid elegance, you must be Zorza," replied Lazimóff.

8

"Indeed, I am. The Centipede I have at my side is Báldur and the Cricket is Saldrím. We are the Kaldáre which you shall be replacing here on this earth," said Zorza.

"I speak for myself and perhaps on behalf of my fellow travellers, when I say that it is a great pleasure for us to be in the presence of such esteemed sorcerers," said Lazimóff.

"I see that your reputation for flattery is well founded, young Lazimóff. The elders have spoken very highly of you in our visions," replied Báldur.

Sensing the presence of the three Butterflies looking on in mild irritation at not having been greeted first, Múzlak turned to them in a graceful and reassuring manner.

"Forgive us, good sirs. It has been a long voyage and our manners seemed to have deserted us somewhere along the Northern Sea," explained Múzlak.

"You have spoken like a true diplomat, young Kaldára. Allow me to introduce you all to your hosts. Before you stand his grace the Duke of the Golden Port, and his two most trusted counsellors who prefer to remain anonymous," said Saldrím.

"Thank you very much, Saldrím. It is a great personal honour for me and the city as a whole, to welcome the next generation of Kaldáre," said the Duke in a kind, if slightly pompous tone.

"The pleasure is all ours, your Grace," replied Grizwald courteously.

"Alas, I have only come to greet you. I cannot stay to entertain your excellences, for I have some pressing issues to attend to. I will instead leave you in the able company of your fellow Kaldáre, who know the city quite well enough. I bid you farewell and a pleasant onward journey," said the Duke while bowing respectfully to his guests, before departing swiftly into the air with a beat of his wings.

"I could feel the pomposity flowing through him," muttered Múzlak dryly.

"You will find such behaviour commonplace throughout these lands, young Múzlak. Do not expect all your visits to be received in the friendliest of fashions," warned Saldrím sternly.

"Alas, it is so. But enough talk of presumptuous aristocrats. It is almost time for us to leave, and we need to impart what little wisdom we have onto you, before we finally set sail home," said Zorza.

———◆≋◆———

So, many hours passed while the six Kaldáre prepared the ship for its next voyage, and discussed at great length the experiences of the older sorcerers over the course of a thousand years. Indeed, the young replacements looked on in astonishment at the tales which their predecessors told them. After all, the time that Báldur, Zorza and Saldrím had spent on this continent, had been eventful to say the least. Stories of luxurious banquets in the halls of multiple monarchs also coincided with dangerous and almost deadly encounters with a plethora of gigantic savage beasts in the wilder parts of the world.

"Your time on this earth has been productive, I dare say," said Múzlak in admiration.

"A fair description of our stay it is indeed, young Múzlak. I do not regret a single moment spent here among these wonderful and fascinating creatures," replied Zorza.

"I couldn't agree more with my fellow Kaldára. I think we can all depart these lands with the sensation of having served the Order well," said Saldrím.

"Indeed, the manner in which the general peace has been kept is most remarkable, your eminences. However, as you have so explained eloquently before, challenges remain," said Grizwald.

"You speak words of wisdom, young Grizwald. All is not well, despite our triumphalism. There are minor rumblings of discontent that need to be dealt with," said Báldur sternly.

"Báldur is right. The issues we have discussed must be resolved as swiftly as possible. The Butterflies of the Dead Mountains have been wishing to break away from Moriátin's rule for quite some time. However, it is only been in these last few months that violence has escalated into something very serious. To the east, the grand old Snail realm of Karlún is on its last knees, and crippled by corruption and infighting. While to the north, the fragile peace between the Spiders and the Flies is close to breaking, and the threat of war looms over them once more," said Zorza.

"Hardly a prelude to full-scale war, though," said Lazimóff dismissively.

"Never underestimate the power of these Insects for self-immolation, young Kaldára," replied Saldrím.

"What is to be done then?" asked Grizwald, with the nervousness of a small infant before a teacher.

"Do what you have been trained to do, Grizwald. Go each your separate ways. Take the roads to the realms in question, and fulfil the work of our order," said Zorza.

"As you wish, your excellences," replied Múzlak respectfully.

With the white vessel finally ready to depart, the young Kaldáre let their predecessors take up their positions to guide their ship northwards. However, just before they could set sail, Grizwald called their attention one more time.

"Is there something else that troubles you, young Kaldára?" inquired Saldrím.

"There is but one more doubt which I currently possess: what has become of the Erkúns in recent times? Nothing can be sensed from the Island, and our power cannot reach the depths of the Underworld," said Grizwald.

"The Erkúns remain as subdued as they have ever been since the signing of the Peace of the Tiba. The conditions of the treaty are being obeyed impeccably and there is no need to quarrel with them. If there is one doubt which I would have, it would be their young Ambassador on the Surface of Insectdom: a creature by the name of Akran Súr. A sly and ambitious one, he is. Despite this, I wouldn't worry too much. The Council of Erkúns keep him on a tight leash. Nevertheless, you must never forget one important thing my dears: never trust an Erkún," advised Zorza.

"Understood," said Múzlak respectfully.

"Farewell, my young friends, and we wish that your time on this earth may be as fruitful as ours. Until we meet again on the shores of the Island," said Báldur warmly, while waving with one of his limbs, in unison with his fellow Kaldáre.

With those final words, the three old Kaldáre ordered their ship to move, and slowly did it glide away from its mooring, through the bay and out into the open ocean and with the Sun setting to the west of them. The young sorcerers were now perfectly aware of the tasks which lay ahead of them.

⁂

Their roles had already been decided. At the crack of dawn Lazimóff was to head southwards to the Grey Mountains to parley with the Butterfly rebels there. Grizwald would head to Nalgála, the capital of Moriátin to speak with the Butterfly Queen. Once decisions had been taken, the three Kaldáre (Grizwald was provided with a Woodlouse as steeds by the Butterflies) would meet at the Bridge of Elubí over the mighty River Tiba. Meanwhile, Múzlak would head eastwards to speak to the monarchs of those troubled lands. It would be a long road for all of them. A long, glorious era had come to an end. A new, if uncertain one, was about to begin.

Chapter 2

The Uncertain King

I t was at the crack of dawn, when Julius rose from his bed and adorned himself with his elegant white robes. Once dressed, the Snail proceeded to his sizeable balcony overlooking the banks of the eternally calm River Anozáth which divided the great city of Sarandos, and contemplated the challenges which would lie ahead for him in the coming days. The young Insect had always found it difficult to sleep, even in his infancy. Although, he could perhaps be forgiven this time for his lack of sleep, taking into account that only yesterday he had been crowned King of Karlún.

The oldest realm of Snails in Insectdom, founded more than four thousand years ago by Julius' ancestors, this kingdom had traditionally been a powerful presence in the eastern lands of Insectdom, between the Maggot fiefdoms to the south and the Snails of Thámrod to the north. Indeed, such was the combative nature of the Snails of Karlún, that even when they were conquered by the mighty Empire of the Red Banner thousands of years, they were never entirely subdued.

The latter information is particularly relevant as this now defunct Insect superpower was founded by the race of Beetles many millennia ago. For centuries almost three quarters of

Insectdom was ruled by the Beetle Emperors from their capital city Amrat and their red banners, leaving a hegemonic cultural, economic, legal and philosophical legacy which outlived the empire's collapse (the most important being their language, which is known today commonly as Insect speech). Indeed, there was almost no Insect realm which did not base its culture and laws at least partially on those established by Amrat.

The constant resistance against the Empire of the Red Banner was a source of pride to the Snails of Karlún, and became part of their folklore. In later years their capital city of Sarandos was often referred to in ancient times as the jewel of the East, with its white buildings and the imposing columns which held up many of the structures within this old city. Its strategic location on the River Anozáth made it the only viable crossing from north to south in the eastern lands, and enriched itself immensely as a result of the extensive trade which took place there. In the days of old the armies of Karlún swept aside all those before them, expanding the realm's borders to the edges of the southern frozen land of Gorgán itself and the borders of Nárim, even capturing the historical Maggot metropolis of Ashúr to the east on more than one occasion. Oh indeed what glorious days those were.

King Julius however, was not inheriting the mighty kingdom of old. Over the last five hundred years, Karlún had been sliding further and further into permanent decline, fatally wounded by the crippling infighting and corruption of its elites, and the ever growing power of the rival Snail realm Thámrod to the north. Its territories consisted nowadays of little more than the eastern banks of the River Anozáth and the barren wastelands of the Desert of Karlún: hardly the most economically beneficial of territories, even if it did provide a useful natural barrier against potential foes from the north.

While the decline had begun long ago, the last twenty two years had been particularly dreadful for Karlún. King Robert the fourth (Julius' late father) had proven to be a particularly wretched monarch. He had been a creature consumed by his own vanity, and possessed a particularly vicious temper, much to the misfortune of many Snails. Yet all the more troubling for the Karlúnian Aristocracy however, was the late monarch's complete lack of interest in state affairs. He preferred instead to empty the realm's coffers in pointless, vainglorious projects such as the construction of enormous golden statues of himself and temples to the Gods, while many of his subjects starved. So notorious was Robert, that he was derided both at home and abroad as the "Robert the Deranged".

The death of the mad monarch came as a great relief to many of his subjects, save those courtiers who had enriched themselves immensely thanks to their slavish obedience, rather than their merit. The coronation of Robert's only living son, proved to be a dull, sombre affair by the standards of Karlúnian kings (a small private ceremony in the Royal palace in the presence of only the most important political elites of the realm). Julius ascended to the throne of Karlún in a particularly delicate situation. The finances of the kingdom were in tatters, food shortages and disease were ravaging Sarandos. More disturbingly still for the new monarch however, was his fear of a potential revolt being organised by certain sectors of the army, fearing that the new King would soon display a similar despotic cruelty which had characterised the rule of his father.

This new monarch however, was a rather different proposition to his predecessor. A much physically smaller Snail than his father, Julius did not exactly look like a King. His small pale frame and his big blue eyes did not exactly inspire much confidence. Indeed, he had only become sovereign thanks to the murder of his older sister by their deranged father, who had strangled her in her sleep after fearing that she had been possessed by a demon who wished to seize his throne.

Fearing for his life, the adolescent Snail fled Sarandos had taken refuge in a remote temple in eastern Karlún, living among the monks who resided there, who in turn taught him how to read and write. Only his long-suffering mother knew of his presence there, thanks to the secret letters he sent her. Once his father was dead however, Julius could return to Sarandos, and claim the throne which now rightfully belonged to him.

Under a calm exterior, the young Snail possessed a fierce ambition. Indeed, he was privately consumed by a burning desire to restore his realm to what he saw as Karlún's rightful place as one of the major powers of Insectdom, and perhaps even to surpass the achievements of his ancestors. Like many Karlúnians, Julius possessed an almost visceral loathing of Thámrod. Their continuous advances on Karlún's borders were provocative. It was as if the northern realm were deliberately teasing its weaker and more decrepit southern neighbour out of spite and rancour. Oh if only those brigands could be put in their place, thought Julius wishfully.

They would not act so smugly once their golden capital city of Elén and their whole fertile kingdom were under the control of Karlún. Nevertheless, for all the young King's dreams of a vast eastern empire, he was no fool. He was perfectly aware of the weakness of his realm, and the strength of his enemies. He would need to bide his time, and once his people were ready, he would strike.

———◆❧◆———

It was around almost midday, when King Julius had finished his breakfast and had proceeded to deal with the first pressing issues of the day. As was custom in the realm of Karlún, the monarch was to meet representatives of the various social groups of society and provide them with guidance and assurances. In the opulent audience chamber of the Royal Palace, Julius sat on his marble throne and listened to the ills of his subjects, and the counsel of his mentor, Brother Severus: an imposing dark-skinned Snail with beady eyes from the east.

Much to the irritation of the Karlúnian aristocracy, Julius had chosen one of the monks who had raised him in the temple to be his counsel. Such a practice was unheard of in Karlún, whose tradition was that the monarch be advised by the highest members of the nobility, and not some lowly member of a religious order. Such trivial formalities were of little concern to the young King. He needed to demonstrate that he was not his father, and rewarding piety was but one way of doing so. If that caused great offence to the nobility, then so be it. He would in turn, find other ways to reward them.

Much to the relief of Julius, the morning meetings had gone relatively well. The representatives of the Karlúnian peasantry had left the audience chamber in a good mood, after having heard the monarch pledge to reduce taxation on the raw materials needed to make food. After all, there is nothing more dangerous for a monarch than to rule a starving peasantry. As the late Paul the Great, founder of Thámrod once said: "A hungry Insect will have no quarrel in knifing his own sovereign. Keep him well fed however, and he will gladly shed his own blood for the throne." Yet, King Julius did not have time to reflect on the history he had once learned at the temple. The timetable of a King was hectic, and his day was just beginning. His most important audience of the day was yet to come.

"Well, I don't think that meeting went too badly did it, Severus?" said Julius gleefully, while gently stroking one of the arms of throne with his right limb.

"I couldn't agree more, Sire. Although, if I may speak frankly, naming an old Snail my child was perhaps not the most correct protocol," replied Brother Severus dryly. The bluntness of the imposing monk would have seen him lose his head under previous monarchs. Yet Julius admired him for his sincerity, and had picked him as his counsel for that very reason.

"I must speak to my people with the love that they deserve. They must be made to know, that I am not my father," said Julius confidently.

"That may be so, Sire. However, I would strongly recommend avoiding using such paternalist tones with your next guest," warned Severus, with the look a disapproving father would give to his own children. Indeed, such was the closeness of the relationship between them, that in some ways the monk was more of a father to Julius than his own late parent.

"Yes, perhaps you are right. My next guest is the Ambassador of the Underworld, is it not?" asked Julius.

"Indeed it is, Sire. I should warn you however, that you will be facing a formidable diplomat. Erkúns are notoriously good with words. Be mindful as to not be seduced by them," responded Severus.

"Your counsel as always commands obedience, Severus. Bring forth the Ambassador," said Julius, ordering his guards to open the doors of the audience chamber.

Within a flash, four heavily armed guards pulled open the doors of the chamber and introduced the guest to their King.

"His Excellency, Akran Súr: Ambassador of the Underworld!" bellowed one of the Snail warriors.

Out from the main hall and into the audience chamber, stepped forth the King's new guest. Akran Súr, like any other Erkún, was an imposing creature, considerably larger than any Insect. His body, tail and wings were of a dull, black colour. His entire body was covered in thick scales, and his four powerful legs were armed with large, razor sharp claws. His eyes were sunken and yellowy.

He also had the power to transform into a biped whenever he pleased giving him greater movement and mobility, and this very occasion was one for him to be on two legs. He wore a long, dark purple cape, adorned with four golden stars, two per epaulette. Each golden star represented one of the four Erkún clans which in Underworld folklore had united the subterranean races.

Akran Súr however, had little time for mythical tales. He was an impressively charismatic and intelligent creature. Despite coming from a relatively low social background among his kind (he had been born the son of a squire), he had managed to cement his place among the elite of the Underworld through sheer will and hard work, and had now been serving as its Ambassador on Insectdom for more than a century. Yet it was the Erkún's voice, which often mesmerised onlookers. It was deep and imposing, yet strangely seductive. Combining that with charisma and fierce ambition made him a formidable diplomat.

"On behalf the peoples of the Underworld, I wish to congratulate his majesty for his accession to the throne. I am confident that you will make as splendid a King as your late father may the Gods rest his soul," said Akran Súr in his majestic voice, while bowing politely within a few feet of the King.

"I thank you for your kind words, Ambassador. However, your utterings on my late father are far too complementary. A lunatic does not deserve such high praise," responded Julius curtly.

"One creature's lunatic, is another's genius, Sire," said the Erkún.

"Perhaps it is so, Ambassador. What matters trouble you, if I may ask?" asked Julius.

"Taking advantage of our first of hopefully many customary audiences, there is a particularly pressing matter which needs discussing, sire: it is the issue of tribute. As is custom since the signing of the Peace of the Tiba in the days of old, all the realms of Insectdom must pay a monthly tribute of one thousand carts of food and gold to my people. In return, we remain underground and see that your race is not harmed, as agreed with the Kaldáre. However, Karlún's payment has been now delayed for one week, and my superiors grow restless. It is rather difficult to keep hungry creatures under control in such circumstances," explained Akran Súr.

"The matter is indeed of great concern, Ambassador. However, your request comes at a bad time. Food production in my realm is undergoing considerable difficulty, and the state's coffers are not exactly overflowing with gold, thanks to my father's inconsiderate spending habits," replied Julius.

"We were all indeed aware of your father's financial mismanagement, sire. However, the law is the law, and thus must be obeyed. It is through this, that we have been able to maintain peace for nine hundred years, and a well-earned one at that," said Akran Súr, with a more serious tone this time.

"I am sorry, Ambassador but I cannot magically conjure up one thousand carts. I am afraid I will need you to tell your superiors to be patient. The carts will be ready, that I can promise. However, it will not be for another month," explained Julius.

"A King must always find a way to fulfil his part of a bargain, no matter the difficulties. If Karlún's payment is not fulfilled, then we will have to find other ways of extracting it. These lands are full of brigands, you know. You never know just what might happen to your trade routes," said the Erkún, with a mischievous grin.

"Is that a threat, Ambassador?" asked Severus sternly.

"Oh of course I am not threatening you, good sirs! The Termite gangs are wild beasts, uncontrollable and answer to no-one. Why would they listen to Erkún?" replied Akran Súr.

"It is profoundly unethical of a diplomat, to insult and threaten his host," said Julius.

"If I have offended you, Sire, then I sincerely apologise. I only wish for us to solve this little problem of ours. Perhaps we could come to some arrangement, your Majesty? Although sincerely, I would prefer to offer it to you in private," explained Akran Súr, in a more diplomatic tone.

"Very well, Ambassador. Severus, I will talk with the Ambassador outside on the balcony. Wait here," said Julius, glancing over at the monk.

"As you wish, Sire," said Severus, bowing respectfully.

The King and the Ambassador then proceeded to walk towards the balcony, and once outside the negotiations could truly begin.

"Forgive me, Sire. I prefer to have this conversation in private. What I am going to say could be considered troubling in the presence of others," said Akran Súr.

"I am listening, Ambassador," replied Julius.

"Word has reached my ears, of a plot against you, Sire. There are rumblings of discontent in the realm. There are nobles and generals who wish to see you fall," explained the Erkún, whispering in the monarch's ear.

"How do you know this?" said Julius.

"It is not through uttered words, that I have become aware of this," said Akran Súr.

"What do you mean, Ambassador?" asked Julius.

"Kaldáre are not the only creatures, who have the gift of mind reading," said Akran Súr.

"How do I know that you not looking to deceive me?" said Julius, doubting the sincerity of the Erkún.

"It is not in my interest, or in the Underworld's to deceive one of our main benefactors," replied Akran Súr.

"If I may ask, who are these individuals?" asked the king inquisitively.

"It would be unwise of me to reveal the names. After all, I do not wish to see creatures die for actions they have not even committed yet," replied Akran Súr.

"Then why do you tell me this?" asked Julius.

"Knowing the existence of this discontent, will help you prepare future decisions more wisely. In any case, that is not the most important matter I wanted to discuss with you. In fact, I'd rather talk over a potential proposition that I was hoping to share with you," said the Erkún.

"I am listening, Ambassador," said Julius, unsure just what exactly this mischievous creature wanted.

"It is the issue of the payment of tribute, Sire. As your realm is quite clearly incapable of paying it on time, I believe we can come to some form of alternate arrangement," explained Akran Súr.

"What sort of arrangement?" asked Julius, uncertainty clouding his judgement.

The Erkún once again approached the young Snail and whispered in his ear "I see your mind, Sire. I am aware of your private ambitions. I know that you wish to restore the former glory of your realm, and to rule all the lands of the east. Between you and me, it would be both a bold and fruitful situation, were it to come to pass. That is why, I am willing to aid you to fulfil your dream," explained Akran Súr.

"Why would the Underworld want to come to my aid? How would you or your people benefit from this?" asked Julius, looking slightly puzzled.

"We are prohibited from ruling the lands on the surface. That does not mean we cannot give counsel to those who seek to do it. In this case, an arrangement would be most beneficial to both parties," replied Akran Súr.

"What exactly do you wish to offer me, Ambassador? Could you please be more specific?" asked Julius, becoming slightly irritated at the constant machinations of this eloquent wordsmith.

"I intend to arrange an audience between yourself and my masters, to discuss a renegotiation of the relations between the realm of Karlún and the Underworld. In return we shall aid you in your ambitions," explained the Erkún.

"Why should I seek to negotiate with the Erkúns? I could easily have a similar conversation with the Kaldáre on the matter," said Julius defiantly.

"The Kaldáre seek only to counsel in their interest. They have great power, but use it only to preserve their own influence. They have no intention of helping the peoples of Insectdom. For example, Kaldáre cannot offer you armies. My people can," said Akran Súr.

"Your superiors are willing to provide Karlún with armies?" asked Julius perplexed.

"For the right price, they will. However, first I must put forward this case to my masters. I am confident that they will agree with me. I am not asking you to accept the offer, Sire. I am merely asking you to consider it," replied Akran Súr.

After several minutes of deep thought, Julius decided to give his guest the best answer he could, albeit with considerable reservations.

"Should your masters agree with your proposal, I will be more than happy to meet them. I am not exactly spoilt for choice at the moment," said Julius.

"Excellent. I shall leave at once, and return here within a month. Until we meet again, Sire," said Akran Súr, bowing respectfully before the monarch and proceeded to leave the palace at a brisk pace.

It took Julius several minutes for him to fully digest what he had just agreed with the Ambassador. The offer put forward by the Erkún seemed startling, yet strangely alluring at the same time. Would the Erkúns really be willing to offer Karlún their armies? Yet, the price in return troubled the young King. After all, he did not entirely trust Akran Súr. However, the King was not in a position to turn down such potential offers lightly. Karlún was in a dire strait, and with a restless population that would not be sad to see its monarch toppled. This coming month would be of vital importance for his realm, and he would need all the counsel he could get. The consequences of Julius' next actions could spell either the glory of Karlún, or its very doom.

Chapter 3

The Jewel of the North

The setting of the Sun and its gradual descent into darkness were of no inconvenience to Grizwald in the slightest. Indeed, the Kaldára remained intrigued to experience his now fourth night under the stars in this alien land. Much to his fortune, the impressive blanket of stars was also accompanied tonight by a full moon, further illuminating the fields below. Such wonders of nature were not entirely new to the Praying Mantis. However, this was the first time in his life that he looked up at the night sky at ground level, rather than at the high altitudes of the Lost Island. Such a pleasant view was made all the more satisfactory by the light breeze which was swirling around.

Nevertheless, the fact that Grizwald was travelling out in the open on a Woodlouse on the flat grasslands of northern Moriátin in the hours of darkness just went to prove just how much of an outsider he really was. For no Insect of sound judgement would find him or herself wandering around under the night sky. Such paranoia may seem strange to the foreign visitor. Yet, the local fears were more often than not, well founded. After all, the lands of Insectdom were home to many a wild and ferocious beast which roamed at will in the dark, always looking for an opportunity to pick off a luckless Insect, often many times smaller in size and stature.

Grizwald and his fellow Kaldáre had been warned repeatedly by the Butterflies of the Golden Port before setting off on their separate missions, about the perils of nocturnal travel throughout Insectdom. But after having travelled through the grasslands for three days and nights without interruption, the Praying Mantis had come to the conclusion that the locals were greatly exaggerating the risk posed. Nothing had happened to him so far, and neither could he sense his fellow sorcerers to be in any mortal danger. Then again, although he would not admit it openly, this tranquillity may have been little more than arrogance on the part of Grizwald. In his mind, the beasts of this world could feel his power and had no intention to quarrel with such a powerful being. However, the Kaldára was soon to find out that such a sense of security was to be utterly unfounded.

◆≋◆

It was around two o'clock in the morning, when the young Praying Mantis was to receive the first of many shocks in his time on Insectdom. While continuing his wander across the seemingly limitless grasslands illuminated only by the small green light emitting from the jewel at the tip of his staff, he began to sense that all was not well. He could smell it in the air. The first clue to such a conclusion was in the very wind that was blowing. The gentle breeze which had characterised that night was picking up at a seemingly tremendous pace. As if, something was forcing the air to discomfort the Kaldára.

After a few seconds Grizwald began to hear something else in the wind. Something potentially far more troubling: the sound of wings. Whatever beast was approaching was certainly large, judging by the mere noise it was making on its descent. In the blink of an eye, a gigantic black shape came plummeting out of the night sky at great speed towards the Praying Mantis. Much to his fortune, Grizwald's lightning-quick reflexes allowed him to throw himself to the ground, with the beast's jaws missing him but by a whisker. His steed however, was not so lucky.

Despite the startling ambush, the Kaldára managed to leap to his feet, raised his staff and prepared himself for another onslaught from his mysterious assailant. In a matter of moments, he found himself face to face with the beast that had decided to torment him on this most pleasant of nights. Circling above, were not one, but three gigantic Bats, their beady eyes fixed upon their prey.

Many were the times that Grizwald had heard terrible tales about these fearsome beasts. Yet, this was the first in which he saw them in the flesh. Of all the deadly creatures which inhabited the earth, the Bat was perhaps one of the most feared. For few animals could match its phenomenal speed in the air, and the lethal accuracy of its jaws. Indeed, it was due to the Bat's formidable reputation as a hunter, that no Insect of sane judgement dared venture outside after dark, lest he wished to meet his end engulfed by the fearsome furry mammal.

However, much to the Bats' surprise, Grizwald was no ordinary creature. At a speed unmatched by ordinary beings, the Kaldára stopped them right in their tracks. At exactly the same moment that the creatures were diving towards their prey, they were forced to bank sharply to avoid crashing into a dome of bright white light which had been summoned from the Praying Mantis' staff at lightning quick speed.

"Be gone! You have no place here! Spawn of the abyss!" bellowed Grizwald defiantly.

Being beasts of the dark, the very sight of the light sent the Bats fleeing in different directions, shrieking in agony at having endured such a terrible punishment for their feeble eyes. Indeed, what tales the Bats would tell, if they could talk. Henceforth, they would think twice about assailing a Kaldára in the hours of darkness.

Despite the unexpected nature of the ambush, the whole experience had left the Kaldára largely untroubled. Such was the power bestowed upon the Kaldára, that it would take a far greater menace to startle them. In fact, Grizwald found the experience a tad exhilarating. A taste of what awaited him during the next millennium in his adventures in these strange new lands.

Roughly an hour later after his close encounter with the Bats, the Kaldára came upon a perfect spot to spend the remainder of the night. In the middle of the vast open grasslands, stood a solitary oasis of around two dozen or so oak trees. The isolated nature of this island of bark in a sea of grass, appealed greatly to the Praying Mantis, who swiftly found a suitable tree in the centre of the oasis, with a hole large enough for him to comfortably lie in. In a matter of minutes, Grizwald dozed off to sleep and off he went in to the world of the unconscious.

Unlike Insects, Kaldáre did not dream, and who instead relived their past memories, and saw into the future. In the case of Grizwald, he was reliving the time as a young infant in which he first became aware of his power. Like all his fellow sorcerers, Grizwald was not born to a family, but simply came into existence:

a fact that seemingly gave credence to the theory among Insects that the Kaldáre were actually Gods who came down from the heavens and incarnated in flesh. Alas, such a question will almost never certainly be answered, even by the very wisest of the world. As powerful as the Kaldáre could be, the possibility of them being deities was deeply unlikely.

Two days had passed since the Bat incident. Much to the disappointment of the Kaldára, no other beast tried to attack him during that time. Instead he found the remainder of his journey to be almost dull in nature. It was around nine o'clock in the morning when Grizwald was finally in visible distance from the great city of Nalgála: known by many in these parts as the jewel of the north.

At first glance, it was certainly a capital fit for a kingdom, nay even an empire. It was a gigantic city, one of the greatest in the world. It gleamed in the sunlight, for its buildings were built from a white stone that was as bright as moonlight itself. Aside from the almost heavenly glow, the city also stood out for its geographical location. For it was built upon a great lake, connected by mighty stone bridges and a network canals accessible only by boat.

Yet despite the peaceful looking appearance of this city, it was certainly not vulnerable. For a great palisade wall encircled the city, with countless guard towers manned by infantry and archers, and dozens of mighty catapults. Such a heavily fortified defensive line was logical in many aspects. After all, the spectre of war hangs permanently over the realm and the memories of the last great conflict do not die easily in these parts.

When the Kaldára stood before the main entrance to the city, he was pleased to see that the wooden gates swung open without the guards even asking who stood before their capital. Such an eventuality did not come as a surprise to him, for he had been in contact with the Queen of Moriátin via meditation for several days now. His presence had been expected for some time.

At a gentle pace he wandered through the perfectly smooth pavements of the city looking for the Royal Palace located within the capital. As in the Golden Port, the local Butterflies looked upon the Praying Mantis in a perplexed manner. It soon became clear that Nalgála was an entirely different beast to settlements previously seen on his travels. This was a city, which oozed wealth. Here it was the norm to wear the most extravagantly coloured tunics possible, so as to impress passers-by.

Such blatant narcissism hardly came as a surprise to Grizwald, taking into consideration that Nalgála was probably home to the highest number of nobles per square metre in Moriátin. For no Butterfly of high birth, was complete without a permanent residence in this jewel of a city.

———◆≈◆———

It was early evening when the Kaldára finally reached the royal palace. It was certainly the largest and most beautiful of all the structures of the city. Its white stone foundations were lavishly decorated with the royal green and white banners of the kingdom, while lush green gardens encircled the building. It also possessed numerous balconies, so that those fortunate enough to enter the palace would have the pleasure of enjoying the splendid views of both the city and the neighbouring lands. The palace was surrounded by the royal guards, and this time Grizwald did have to explain to the soldiers who he was and why he sought an audience with the Queen.

Once the Praying Mantis walked through the main doors he came across the main hall of the palace. Like any other building in Nalgála, sunlight poured in through the ceiling illuminating every nook and cranny of the place. Yet unlike other settlements in the city, the palace was richly decorated with stunningly beautiful marble, for even the staircase was forged of this precious stone. The circular hall also had countless statues situated all around, encircling those who wandered in. These sculptures were of the Kings and Queens of old, long gone, but not forgotten by the people of Moriátin. Grizwald was welcomed at the foot of the great staircase by two Butterflies awaiting their guests, one male and one female.

"Welcome to Nalgála, oh mighty Grizwald," said the female Butterfly in a calm, yet authoritative voice.

"Thank you very much, your Majesty. Your hospitality is most welcome," replied Grizwald.

The level of respect being shown by Grizwald towards his host was appropriate, taking into account he was before Queen Alessandra herself, sovereign of Moriátin. At first glance she certainly looked like a Queen. A tall, elegant Insect, dressed in dark red robes and with large black and yellow wings, and wearing a long sword on her left hand side. Yet for her undoubtedly pleasant appearance, the Kaldára was aware he was standing before a formidable monarch. It was her sparkly, blue eyes that most impressed him, and it was hard not to be transfixed by them. For they looked sharp, and the monarch's very stare exuded intelligence.

After all, one could not be ruler of a great kingdom for nearly forty Insect years as in the case of Alessandra, and not possess a brilliant mind. Under her stewardship the realm was as wealthy as ever, and was undoubtedly one of the world's greatest powers, indeed perhaps the greatest of them all. As for her personal situation, her lack of spouse was attributed in some social circles to her strong character and her unwillingness to submit herself to the whims of a husband. More cynical observers whispered that this was due to her inherent dislike of many Butterfly nobles and a long relationship with one of her bodyguards: a Butterfly of low birth, and therefore an unacceptable choice of spouse for a monarch.

After a brief introduction, Grizwald came to realise that the male Butterfly at the side of the Queen, was Yanis, the Duke of Elénluin: the monarch's uncle. As ruler of the second largest city in Moriátin, the noble was one of the most powerful Butterflies of the realm. His elder brother Francis had previously ruled for thirty two Insect years until his untimely death on a state visit in the jaws of a Bat. While the Duke had always privately craved the throne, he was fiercely loyal to his niece and somewhat of a father figure to her and her two younger brothers ever since the death of Francis.

The Duke was of a similar colour to his niece, yet of a considerable smaller stature. Dressed entirely in a black robe and armed with a long sword, the noble cut a rather intimidating figure. The stern manner which he spoke did little to dispel the authoritarian aura which he possessed in abundance.

"It is a great pleasure to finally meet you in person, Grizwald. I have always found Kaldáre to be good company," said the Duke.

"I shall do my utmost to avoid the breaking of that fine tradition then, Your Grace" replied Grizwald courteously.

"It is a long road from the Golden Port to the capital. I presume you must be quite weary and famished," said Alessandra.

"Alas, that is so, your Majesty. At this moment in time, I am in need of a little nourishment," explained Grizwald wearily.

"Then no time must be wasted. Join us for dinner now, and let us talk about a great number of things, over a fine meal and in intelligent company," suggested Alessandra.

"Couldn't have put it better myself, your Majesty," agreed the Duke, as humourless as ever.

———◆≋◆———

Darkness had finally fallen over Nalgála, when the three great statesmen had finished their extravagant meal on one of the balconies overlooking the great sights of the city, in the company of multiple soldiers and servants. The generous offerings had left the Kaldára profoundly grateful, albeit with a very full stomach. Nevertheless, he put his mild physical discomfort to one side, and once pleasantries were over, it was time to get down to business.

"As pleasant as it is to receive a mighty Kaldára such as yourself in our company, you have yet to reveal in person the purpose of your visit. Why have come to us, Grizwald?" inquired the Queen with a slightly stern look on her face.

"You are indeed right, your Majesty. It would be inappropriate of me to take advantage of your marvellous hospitality, without revealing the motive of my visit. I am fully aware of the conflict that engulfs Moriátin. I come here as an ambassador, to mediate between the warring parties in your realm, as an arbiter between Nalgála and the rebels of the Dead Mountains," explained Grizwald.

"There is nothing to discuss on the matter. The rebels are insolent filth and shall be dealt with accordingly," remarked the Duke in a slightly irritated tone.

"Alas, as crude and uncompromising as it sounds I share similar feelings to my uncle on the matter. I am not aware how much your predecessors have told you," said Alessandra.

"They mentioned briefly the existence of a rebellion to the south, and little more. I must confess, that my ignorance on the issue is considerable," said Grizwald, slightly embarrassed.

"The union of Moriátin with the Butterflies of the Dead Mountains is an old one, more than four hundred Insect years at that. Having being reduced to bankruptcy thanks to their own incompetence and countless wars with the Moths of Nárim, the mountain folk came to us for aid. That generous assistance was given by my forebears, in exchange for loyalty, which in turn was duly given. Yet, as the decades passed, the Butterflies of this region became ever more demanding and its nobles more difficult to deal with. Four years ago on this very day, they officially broke their oath of loyalty and declared unilateral independence from our realm. Our armies have been locked in combat with them since then," explained the Queen in a serious tone.

"This is all the more reason for negotiations to take place, your Majesty. Four years of bloodshed is enough for any realm to take. None more so than in a divided kingdom," replied Grizwald.

"Your intentions are noble, wise Kaldára. However, I am afraid that I must emphasise that they are misplaced. We do not look too kindly on traitors, least of all those who break their oaths, and slaughter our own kin," said the Duke grimly.

"Is this true, your Majesty?" asked Grizwald.

"Alas, it is. The Butterfly in question was my younger brother, Prince Cecil. He was slain almost a year ago by the rebel filth. The pain of his passing has still not washed away," replied Queen Alessandra in a sombre tone.

"I cannot but imagine the suffering that this loss has caused. Despite, I feel that something must be done to halt this madness," said Grizwald.

"It shall be done, Grizwald. I can guarantee you that. Once I have the rebel leaders hanging from the highest trees," growled the Duke.

"I beseech you, your Majesty. At this very moment my fellow Kaldára Lazimóff is venturing south to parlay with the rebels. Being neutral foreigners, perhaps both parties will look upon us with less hostility. The war will not end with ever more severe reprisals. The more a population is repressed, the more desperate and vicious it becomes. Alas, the line between a strong ruler and a tyrant, is very thin, your Majesty. At least offer Lazimóff the chance to talk sense in to them," argued Grizwald.

Tensions were in danger of running high momentarily during the discussions. Despite his best efforts to restrain his emotions, the Duke of Elénluin had grown weary of the Kaldára's obstinacy, and only his niece prevented him from unleashing his full fury upon their guest. Several moments passed before anyone uttered another word, and in the end, it was the turn of the Queen herself to break the uncomfortable silence.

"My heart finds the idea of parlaying, revolting to say the least. Nevertheless, my mind concurs with your arguments. By royal decree I shall postpone hostilities momentarily, in order to grant your fellow Kaldára safe passage through the war zone. I will empower you both to offer the following concessions to the rebel leaders: should they lay down their arms immediately, I will approve a further increase in legislative powers for their region, regarding taxation and religious observance. In return I will allow them to present me their offers. If no compromise is made, then I must regretfully resume hostilities. This is all I can offer you now," explained Queen Alessandra.

"You have chosen wisely, your Majesty. In the name of the Gods, I will do my utmost to bring peace to your realm," replied Grizwald gratefully.

"In the name of the Gods, I pray that you are right," answered the monarch.

———◆☙◆———

Two days later the Kaldára departed from the luxurious confines of Nalgála and headed south to meet Lazimóff at the Bridge of Elubí, once the Bumble Bee had returned from the Dead Mountains. As he lay in bed the night before his voyage, the Praying Mantis reflected on the magnitude of the task at hand. It was one thing to have convinced the Queen that his plan was viable. To persuade her whole realm would only be possible if he succeeded.

The Queen's reluctant acceptance of his proposal seemed heavenly in comparison with the thinly veiled hostility shown by her uncle and a great number of the other high ranking nobles at the royal court. For all their outward politeness, he sensed the scorn and the scepticism in the minds of these powerful Insects in the presence of their sovereign as she explained the proposals to them in person the morning after their soirée.

Such contempt for his peace proposals made Grizwald all the more determined to succeed in his venture. If not for the sceptical elites of Moriátin and the Dead Mountains, then for the thousands of poor souls who would lose their lives in the brutal torment of battle were he to fail.

38

Chapter 4

The Council of Erkúns

The harsh volcanic lands west of Karlún have never been renowned for their natural beauty, and are certainly not the easiest to pass on foot. However, one holds a different perspective if these lands can be bypassed by flying. Akran Súr and his ilk were but of a handful of sentient creatures that possessed such a precious ability. Indeed, the world seemed so small when seen from above, almost insignificant perhaps.

Yet, it was not the view from above which was occupying the mind of the Erkún at this moment in time. Over and over again, the Ambassador remembered the words he had exchanged with the young King of Karlún. He was surprised at how easy it had been to talk to the newly crowned monarch. The Snail's relative humility in particular, was something which struck the Erkún. So accustomed to dealing with narcissistic, capricious monarchs throughout the world, exchanging words with Julius on the other hand proved to be a rather pleasurable experience.

However, the conversation with the monarch would seem relatively straightforward in comparison to the one which would now await the Ambassador. It was one thing for King Julius to accept his proposal, but convincing the leaders of the Underworld would be another matter entirely. Indeed, the ruling body of the realm below, known as the Council of Erkúns was notoriously conservative and hostile to radical change. Convincing them would a great challenge for Akran Súr. Yet such was confidence in his own ability as a diplomat that in his eyes, there was no obstacle which could stop him from getting his way.

After a full day of flying, the Erkún finally reached his destination in the early hours of the evening. At first sight, from above it seemed as though he was going to land in the middle of a seemingly impassable labyrinth of razor sharp rocks, standing alone in the barren lands west of Karlún. Hardly the most ideal of landing sites, one could say. This hostile gathering of stone was almost impassable on foot, due to the rough terrain and the confusing pathways which ran through it. However, from the air Akran Súr was perfectly aware of what he was seeking in this perilous maze.

Having swiftly landed in the middle of the only clearing among these rocks, he then headed towards the very heart of the labyrinth. At first glance, there seemed to nothing of substance to see, barring a gigantic circular stone perfectly embedded within the earth, four or five times wider than the Erkún himself. Nevertheless, at closer inspection, the Ambassador could see exactly what he sought: four distinctive markings, carved into the rock, representing four golden stars. To an outsider, these symbols would mean very little, but to an Erkún they were sacred. These stone markings were a password to open the Gala Gún: the door of the Underworld.

Suddenly, Akran Súr began to utter some incomprehensible sounds in his native Erkún Tongue (a bizarre form of hissing to those unused to speaking or hearing that form of speech) and rocked his head slightly back. His normally black throat began to glow a fierce orange colour and within a split second a barrage of flame erupted from the Erkún's mouth, and he proceeded to direct the fire with his neck onto the stone markings, until they were all totally engulfed by the flames.

Several seconds later, the Erkún stood back as the ground began to shake and the circular stone began to transform itself. The rock split open into four separate sections which gradually rose up from the earth and stood up vertically. With the door of the Underworld now open, Akran Súr proceeded to move towards the edge of the gaping hole which now lay before him. Awaiting the Erkún was a seemingly bottomless pit consumed in almost total darkness, with only a faint fiery glow visible at the very bottom. Such a forbidding sight would have sent shivers down the back of any terrestrial being, but not so the Ambassador. He simply left himself fall into in the darkness, spreading his wings while plummeting downwards at a great speed.

After almost ten seconds of lightning quick flight down the dark pit, the Erkún landed on the surface at the bottom with an almighty thump. Just exactly where he had landed, would have seemed horrific for any creature which lived on the surface. The Underworld was a dark, forbidding place which struck for its hideous appearance. The terrain was incredibly harsh, little more than ash and rocks. The only visible light in this forbidding realm came from the multiple lava flows which dotted the landscape.

Crossing this inhospitable terrain was only possibly thanks to the multiple black, stone bridges which had been magically forged by the Erkúns long ago.

Almost by instinct, Akran Súr headed northwards, towards the very heart of the Underworld itself. Despite the lifeless appearance of this terrible place, life did exist here. Indeed, within a few minutes Akran Súr came across members of his fellow species going about their business among the rocks. However, these Erkúns were of a lower caste to the Ambassador and proceeded to bow respectfully before him once they became aware of his presence.

Akran Súr pitied the poor wretches and secretly despised the tradition of castes and hierarchies which still dominated both on the surface and in the Underworld. After all, he had risen from the bottom to the top, and had endured first -hand experience of the scorn and derision of higher born Erkúns. Oh, if only the insolent snobs who had taunted him in his youth lived to see him now, he often thought to himself.

———◆❧◆———

After almost an hour of travel, Akran Súr was getting very close to where the Council of Erkúns traditionally met. This venue was a gigantic barren rock surrounded by an imposing lake of lava, accessible only by a solitary black bridge. However, the Ambassador would not head there quite just yet. He needed to meet someone of great importance before gracing his masters with his presence. Thankfully, this individual had heard Akran Súr's call. Standing before the bridge waiting for the Ambassador, was a bizarre looking two-legged creature, with only two arms and a pair of black wings.

While considerably smaller than a Erkún, it would still seem imposing to an outsider. This particular being was concealed in a suit of heavy looking, silver armour, and wearing a long sword in a black scabbard on its left hand side. In its armoured right hand it carried a large fearsome looking helmet adorned with two mighty horns and with only a thin visor as means of providing vision. Yet, it was not this formidable looking armour which would have disturbed Insects the most. It was the creature's head which inspired fear above all. It possessed no discernible facial features of which to speak of. Indeed, it was only a skull, consumed by a permanent bright green flame.

This terrifying beast was a member of the so-called Blood Brotherhood. The adherents of this ancient warrior order were descended from an Underworld race known as the Mosquitoes, notorious for their insatiable lust for the blood of others. Since the dawn of time, the greatest of these creatures have been hand-picked by the Erkúns on the Council to serve as their personal bodyguards and as commanders of their armies. In order to prolong their naturally short lives, the Erkúns mutate their bodies to such a degree that they would be deemed unrecognisable to their loved ones. These Mosquitoes would never age, feel no pain and possess a limited magical power of their own.

However, this dark power comes at a terrible price. The Mosquitoes which serve in the Blood Brotherhood are slaves to their masters, deprived of all personal thought and freedom, and bound in life and death with their owners. The level of control is such that these wretched beings even lose their own names. This particular member of the Brotherhood served Akran Súr, simply because as Ambassador he was entitled to have one. Like all his peers on the Council, Akran Súr had no knowledge or interest in his bodyguard's origins, and merely called him the Dead Knight, because of his lifeless appearance.

"Greetings, Master," said the Dead Knight in a deep, forbidding voice, while bowing respectfully.

"Thank you very much for answering my call, my friend," replied Akran Súr politely in Insect speech.

"What is your will, Master? What is required of me?" asked the Dead Knight, never daring to look directly into the eyes of his master.

"All shall be revealed very shortly. Firstly, I must address my superiors at the Council. Follow me, my friend," said Akran Súr, guiding his servant with one of his enormous limbs.

Having swiftly crossed the bridge, the Erkún and his bodyguard proceeded to advance towards the centre of the island. The Council of Erkún was already in place waiting in their stone seats for the meeting to begin, surrounded by a circle of heavily armed members of the Blood Brotherhood, and who let the Ambassador through once they realised who he was. As per tradition in the Underworld, the Council was composed of six members, who in turn would conduct the meeting in Erkún Tongue. Four of these members were direct representatives of the four main Erkún clans (northern, southern, eastern, and western) each wearing the colours of their house, as well as the Ambassador and the Emperor of the Underworld.

The current Emperor of the Underworld hailed from the northern clan (Hordar as he was known among his peers) looked and sounded like the powerful ruler that he was. He had been ruling the Underworld for the last century and a half, and was generally respected. He was a creature of mighty stature even among Erkúns, with incredibly broad shoulders and wings. Yet, he was unusual in the sense that he had been born an albino: a white Erkún in a dark world.

He was fortunate that his late father had been an unconventional character among his species and let his unnatural son live. It was normally the custom for Erkúns to drown physically imperfect infants in lava at birth. Being different from his brethren, Hordar had to prove his worth considerably more than others despite being of noble birth. His ferocious determination was legendary among his kind and many were fearful of looking into his pale, blue eyes.

His friendship with Akran Súr had begun long before he had been crowned Emperor. Hordar's late father had previously served as Ambassador on the surface and Akran Súr was appointed as his personal counsellor, after previously serving the Northern clan as a servant. The crafty diplomat was perfectly aware of his protégé's enormous potential and on his death bed he pleaded his son to make Akran Súr Ambassador of the Underworld once he became Emperor, arguing that he sensed a great power in him. Hordar promised to carry out his father's wishes, and he was true to his word. He felt a great connection with Akran Súr in many aspects: two outsiders in a world where social status and physical appearance ruled.

The role of supreme ruler in the Underworld alternated among the clans. When the leader of one clan was made Emperor, he would rule until his death and would then be succeeded by the leader of another. The sixth member of the Council was the Ambassador of the Underworld on the surface. Traditionally, this individual belonged to one of the four clans. Akran Súr however, was the first diplomat in the history of the Underworld not to have come from one of these powerful families. The ambitious

Erkún was a clear outsider, and it often showed in these meetings. The fact that the Emperor had appointed a lower caste Erkún as Ambassador, did not sit well with some of the Council members.

"You're late, Ambassador," said the Southern clan leader coldly, while brushing ash off his red cape with one of his mighty limbs.

"Forgive me my Lords, the meeting in Karlún took a little longer than expected and the weather was not the best for flying," replied Akran Súr courteously, facing only the Emperor and ignoring the Erkún who had scorned him.

"Very well, Ambassador. What tidings do you bring us from the surface?" asked the Emperor inquisitively.

"As the Council requested, I have paid a visit to all the main realms of the surface in order to demand their monthly tribute. All have complied with the rules and their deliveries shall arrive on time. There is however, one kingdom which will not be able to complete its payment on schedule," explained Akran Súr.

"Which realm has been foolish enough not to balance its books properly?" asked the Eastern clan leader.

"That would be the Kingdom of Karlún, my Lord. Its continuing descent into decadence is most troubling," replied Akran Súr.

"Any realm that fails to pay its monthly tribute on time, must suffer the consequences. Those are the conditions of the Peace of the Tiba. Send word to the Termite gangs on the surface. Inform them that the Emperor of the Underworld will reward them greatly if they plunder Karlún," ordered the Emperor glancing over at his peers.

"If I may just have a moment, Sire. In this particular situation, I feel it would be unwise for us to carry out the punishment just yet," said Akran Súr.

"The word of the Emperor is law, Ambassador. Traditions may mean little to you, but they are of vital importance to the clans. How else can we maintain order in the Underworld?" interjected the Western clan leader, looking at the Ambassador with thinly veiled contempt.

"Let the Ambassador speak, my Lord. All opinions must be respected in the Council," said the Emperor sternly.

"Thank you, Sire. I propose an alternative form of extracting what is owed to us by Karlún," said Akran Súr.

"What alternative is this, Ambassador?" asked the Emperor.

"I propose that we make a deal with the young King of Karlún," explained the Ambassador.

"What deal would this be?" asked the Eastern clan leader.

"The King is politically feeble and vulnerable. He is unlikely to survive much longer on the throne unless he takes drastic decisions. I have seen his mind. His ambition is quite unlike anything I have felt in a monarch. Never in all my years as Ambassador, have I seen such a lust for absolute power. He yearns for the creation of an empire encompassing all the lands east of the Tiba, perhaps even beyond that. I propose that we facilitate this by offering him our mighty armies. In return he must pledge his loyalty and his soul to us, while we rule Insectdom," argued Akran Súr, with a sly grin.

The arguments put forward by the Ambassador were greeted with a mixture of derision and laughter from his fellow council members. Yet, this was not a surprise for the charismatic politician. He had foreseen such a reaction. All he needed to do now was to use his powers of persuasion to play to the most important personality traits in most Erkúns: arrogance and an insatiable lust for power.

"What exactly have you been smoking on the surface, Ambassador?" howled the Northern clan leader with absolute derision. Do you really expect us to tear up the Peace of the Tiba, just to satisfy your ridiculous ambitions and your vanity?"

"He is right, Ambassador. To undo the last nine hundred years of our history, would be a fools' errand," said the Emperor sceptically.

"So often I hear of this so-called Peace of the Tiba. But what peace is this? The Kaldáre forced this humiliating treaty upon our ancestors, with nothing but contempt. Our relation with them since then has not been one of equals, but one of master and slave! It almost brings me to tears to think of how bereft of pride our people have become!" exclaimed Akran Súr.

"Choose your words carefully, commoner. They may be your last as Ambassador," growled the Eastern clan leader.

"Enough! Let him speak, my fellow council members," barked the Emperor, fearful of an escalation in tensions.

"Just think for a moment about our current state of affairs, my Lords. We live here condemned to misery and beggary in this barren wasteland, living off scraps given to us as tribute. The Underworld is our home, of that there can be no doubt. Nevertheless, I have seen much of the rest of the world, and I can assure you that it is on Insectdom that we will find our salvation. Oh you should see the world on the surface, my lords! You should see for yourselves the beauty of the grasslands of Moriátin, the mighty forest of Anóg, the spectacular peaks of the Golden Mountains or the deserts of Karlún. We rule over Insects here in the Underworld, so why not here on the surface? All Erkúns would have the possibility to rule over lands they could never have dreamed of. The realms of Insectdom are weak, corrupt and warlike. We possess qualities which their rulers do not: wisdom and discipline," argued Akran Súr forcefully.

"What of the Kaldáre, Ambassador? The surface is their domain. They will not step aside for us to rule in their place," warned the Emperor.

"That is indeed true, sire. But we have one advantage over them: we have imagination. The Kaldáre vermin are fixated on merely conserving their power. They advise only in their own interest and to preserve the status quo. So sure are they of their position on the surface, that they only have three of their kin there presently. They continue to assume that we remain subservient, docile and weak. They are blind, my Lords. We must act swiftly," explained Akran Súr.

"So what are you suggesting, Ambassador? Are we to slay the Kaldáre?" asked the Southern Clan Leader.

"Precisely, and we should also slay all the rulers of Insectdom for good measure. A foe bereft of leadership, is far easier to conquer," answered Akran Súr with a mischievous grin.

These bold words caused the Council to descend into intense discussion, just as the diplomat had foreseen. After having been dormant for so many years, the lust for power which lurked in every Erkún was awoken once more. Everything was going exactly as planned. After several minutes of deliberation, the Erkún leaders turned their attention towards him once more.

"Your schemes are fraught with peril, Ambassador. Nevertheless, your skill with words is unparalleled. A flame of interest now flickers in me," said the Northern Clan leader slyly. Such warm words, gave the ambitious diplomat great satisfaction indeed.

"Your words seem to have taken effect, Ambassador. A vote will now be cast. Those in favour of ending this unjust peace and avenging our ancestors say aye!" exclaimed the Emperor.

His call to vote was answered by a resounding aye by all the members of the Council. Akran Súr grinned mischievously as he watched his fellow council members vote in unison.

"It is now settled then. The Peace of the Tiba is forthwith null and void. It is now we, who shall establish terms upon Insectdom. Come forth, members of the Blood Brotherhood" growled the Emperor, switching to Insect speech.

In response the two dozen or so members of this terrible order abandoned their posts and stepped forward in unison to hear the commands of their Emperor.

"Head to the surface forthwith, my mighty warriors. Divide yourselves into teams of two, head to the capitals of the world, and slay the Kaldáre and the rulers of these realms. Leave no survivors," ordered the Emperor.

"Thy will be done, Sire," replied the Dead Knight.

With the order swiftly given, the Blood Brotherhood set off flying towards the Gala Gún at great speed, armed to the teeth for the task at hand. In turn, the Council of Erkúns concluded its meeting and its members all went their separate ways in the dark abyss that was the Underworld.

As for Akran Súr, he could not avoid feeling a tremendous degree of self-satisfaction. His talent in influencing others remained unbroken and unparalleled. The path to glory for his people was now open and there was no turning back. Nevertheless, the Ambassador did not intend to work on his participation in this great undertaking just yet. Indeed, the diplomat wished above all to see his own family living in the north of the Underworld.

Due to his consistent travelling around the realms of Insectdom, Akran Súr had not laid eyes upon his beloved wife and daughter for almost one year: something which gave him great pain. Taking into account the magnitude and the risk of the plan he had just devised, it seemed wise to the Erkún to see his kin. Indeed, there was no guarantee of success in this venture, and should Akran Súr perish, he at least wanted the assurance of seeing his family one last time, before setting off into the unknown that was the future.

Chapter 5

Eastern Promises

The River Tiba, is without doubt, the most spectacular body of water throughout all of Insectdom. Stretching from the western borders of Moriátin up to the far eastern shores of Skrallog, this mighty river is so wide, that it takes around one Insect week to cross by boat, with currents as wild as those found at sea. Indeed, it is only physically crossable on foot via three gigantic solitary bridges: constructions which were made long ago by the first Kaldáre. Were it not for these imposing crossings forged of magical material, then the northern and southern lands of Insectdom would remain forever apart.

The imposing river however, was of little concern to Múzlak, who had far more pressing issues to reflect on while finishing his flight over the Tiba. For almost a month, the young Kaldára had been travelling, and his flight across the river marked only the halfway mark of his travels. Within a few days, the vast expanse of water was left behind, and replaced by the barren deserts of Karlún.

It was hard not to be awed by the vast expanses of these lands. The landscape was dotted by countless sand dunes of sometimes gigantic stature, as well as multiple rock formations.

Múzlak personally found the lifeless nature of this imposing desert both serene and eerie at the same time. It was some ways the perfect natural defence for the realm of Karlún. Indeed, foreign armies had always found it a troublesome obstacle, resulting in the deaths of many soldiers before even a single battle had been fought. Yet, the further north he travelled, the closer to civilisation he became.

———◆≋◆———

Within four Insect days, he finally reached his first destination. At around ten o'clock in the morning, with no troubling incidents to speak of on his voyage, Múzlak stood before the physical border between Karlún and the rival Snail kingdom of Thámrod: the Eastern Wall. Over one thousand years ago, the rulers of Thámrod at the time decreed that due to the ceaseless wars and invasions between Karlún and Thámrod, the construction of a defensive barrier was of paramount importance, to prevent the pillaging of their lands by their southern rivals. Fifty years after that royal decree, the Eastern Wall was completed, at a great financial and personal cost to the kingdom.

The end product was a defensive structure of breath-taking size. At its highest point, the wall was as tall as a hill, and was built with a white stone that reflected the sunlight. It was not just the height of the wall which was striking, but also the length. From west to east it stretched from the banks of the River Tiba down to the shores of the Eastern Sea. Every inch of this great fortified structure was armed to the teeth. For every Insect mile of wall, there were five fortified towers all equipped with large ballistae and trebuchets. Aside from the mighty weaponry on display, there were tens of thousands of heavily armed Snail soldiers in their dark blue armour on almost semi-permanent watch garrisoned along the entire wall.

In order to avoid being shot on sight by flying over the fortifications, Múzlak decided to land directly in front of the main gate: an imposing iron structure which was almost impossible to break down. Like his fellow Kaldáre, the Dragonfly had made his presence known through contact via meditation with his hosts. As a result, his arrival was known and perfectly welcome. Indeed, the Kaldára did not even have to identify himself, when the great iron-gate swung open.

Once passing the door to Thámrod, Múzlak found himself being greeted by four heavily armed Snails. Out of this imposing group came forth the commanding officer, who addressed the Kaldára with a stern, yet amicable tone.

"Good morning, mighty Kaldára. His Majesty is expecting you in the Royal Fort. Please follow us," explained the Snail officer.

"But of course, my dear sirs," replied Múzlak courteously.

After walking almost half an Insect mile, the five Insects reached the Royal Fort: the stronghold which co-ordinated the Snail defences on the Eastern wall. As with any other construction built to house monarchs, the fort was imposing and ostentatious at the same time. Surrounded by a small moat and reachable only via four bridges forged of white stone under the watchful eye of several thousand Snail soldiers behind the walls, the fort was not easy to breach by any stretch of the imagination. Indeed, no foreign army had ever set foot inside the Royal Fort in all its existence. Like the bridges which surrounded it, the stronghold was built with white stones, with each side adorned with gigantic dark blue banners, with a dark red ruby in the middle.

Having crossed one of the white bridges and walked past the main gate of the fort, Múzlak and his military escort entered a large courtyard teeming with soldiers and civilians going about their daily business. In the very centre, stood the welcoming party which Múzlak had come to parley with, alongside a large fountain. There were exactly eight Insects in total, who stood before the Kaldára. Four of these were Snails (two of which were soldiers), while the other half were of another race: Spiders from the north, half of them also being soldiers.

"Oh mighty Kaldára, it gives me great pleasure to introduce you to his Majesty, King Frederick the Third of Thámrod, his Excellency Viscount Bertrand of the Golden Mountains, his Majesty King Robert the Second of Skrallog, and his advisor Lord Tiberius of Golrum," explained the Snail officer who had first greeted the Kaldára at the foot of the Eastern Wall.

"It is a great honour for me to finally meet you all in person. I trust my messages via meditation have not been too discomforting, your Majesties," said Múzlak respectfully.

"The feeling is mutual, good sir, even if you do seem rather young for a Kaldára," said King Frederick.

"I concur with my dear Snail, albeit with no reservations over your age," said King Robert courteously.

"Age is but a number. Power is permanent, your Majesties," replied Múzlak.

Indeed, the Kaldára was impressed with what he saw before him. The Snail King was of a large stature, his body and shell concealed under long black robes, and a wizened face which exuded intelligence. His grey limbs were adorned with several rings, and attached to his belt was a long sword of with a ruby encrusted hilt. Yet this was no ordinary blade. This was the famous royal sword of Thámrod, forged many thousands of years ago by the Spiders as a gift of friendship to the founder of the northern Snail realm, Paul the Great. A blade so striking in its elegance and beauty, that many called it the finest sword ever forged.

The Viscount by comparison, was a less impressive looking figure in his blue robes, and preferring to remain silent. The only discernible feature of this noble was that he lacked a left limb, presumably lost on some hunting expedition or in battle: something that Múzlak felt would be inappropriate to ask. Yet, it was the Spiders which most impressed the Kaldára. Both the monarch and the lord were gigantic in stature, with eight large black limbs which stuck out of their respective grey and red robes which concealed their impressive bodies.

But above all, it was the size of their heads which most struck Múzlak. One could only imagine the brilliance contained inside those minds, and judging by the spectacular contributions made by the Spiders in the fields of engineering this intelligence was genetic. Even if King Robert looked rather youthful in nature, in comparison to the older and more surly noble to his side.

<hr />

After exchanging pleasantries and a light lunch with a little wine, it was time to get to business. It was decided that it was more appropriate to take these matters inside the royal fort, due to the stifling heat during the afternoon hours. Each monarch wished to convey to the Kaldára the respective situations of their realms, as well as their concerns. For many hours the group of Insects discussed in considerable detail the matters at hand.

Indeed, for Múzlak it was quite an educational experience, for he learnt a great deal about the two realms with which he would have to deal with over the next one thousand years. His elders had mentioned both kingdoms briefly, albeit with the typical subliminal condescension which Kaldáre deemed suitable for normal Insects. He now felt a strong desire to set off into the wild and see for himself the many wonders which these two great people had to offer. He wished to see with his own eyes the Snail city of Elén, which was supposedly made of gold, the great Spider port city of Iscas in the far north, or the towering snowy peaks of the Golden Mountains which separated the Spiders from their Snail neighbours.

Gathering from what Múzlak heard during the meeting, relations between the two races have almost always been extremely cordial. Historically, there had been few wars between the two peoples, who preferred instead to reap the benefits of trade. The Spiders craved the excellent agricultural products of their southern neighbours, while the Snails were very much enamoured with the silk and metals which the northern realm produced in abundance. In any case, both races had bigger fish to fry than each other, as the Kaldára was discovering.

Aside from learning about his hosts' cultures and socio-economic situations, Múzlak learned a great deal about the conflicts which both races were immersed. To the north the Spiders were locked in a semi-permanent struggle with the Flies: a war-like race which had its strongholds up in the Icy Mountains of the far north. So constant were the wars between them that the years of peace were hard to come by. King Robert for example, was the first Spider king in history not to have spent the first three years of his reign locked in battle with the Flies.

Meanwhile, to the south the Snails of Thámrod also had a less than amicable relationship with the kingdom of Karlún. For many centuries the two Snail realms had grappled with each other for supremacy of the east. For many years Sarandos had been the dominant power, even controlling Elén at one point. However, with Karlún now seemingly in permanent decline and the Eastern Wall complete, the most recent rulers of Thámrod slept a little better, knowing that their ancient rival was more of a threat to itself, than to the peoples ruled from Elén.

After hours of fascinating conversation the party left the fortress to watch the Sun set from the wall, alongside the many soldiers which manned its defences. This gift of nature was pleasant to behold. The sight of the great flaming star setting behind the great sand dunes of the desert of Karlún was a spectacular thing to see for any creature fortunate enough to appreciate such natural beauty. It was here upon the mighty white stones which made up the Eastern Wall, where Múzlak could reflect more peacefully on the wave of information which he needed in order to perfect his role as mediator and peace maker in these oriental lands.

"As you can see, Múzlak, our world is racked with many troubles even in times of peace. You will have your work cut out for the next millennium. Of that you can be certain," said King Frederick.

"Indeed, it seems to be so, your Majesty. I may need a lifetime just to help solve the issues affecting your two splendid realms," replied Múzlak wryly.

"Your predecessors were visibly weary at the end of their tenure, despite their best efforts to conceal it. We hope such an eventuality does not come to pass with you, oh great Kaldára," said

King Robert, who was briefly interrupted by Viscount Bertrand, who whispered something inaudible to the Spider monarch.

"I hope so too. Judging by the relative calm between the borders of Thámrod and Karlún, I feel that I should now head northwards to the Icy Mountains to parlay with the Flies," said Múzlak.

"The Flies are a treacherous filth, godless and accursed. They believe in nothing but themselves. In any case Kaldára, you will not be the first magical being to visit them this year," said King Robert.

"The Ambassador of the Underworld, I presume?" asked Múzlak in a more stern tone.

"Indeed. The Flies have always had good relations with the rulers of the Underworld. We have always suspected that they have always been in league with them. However, this current diplomat denies it vehemently and has acted frequently as a mediator between Spiders and Flies," explained King Robert.

"He has always struck me as a curious individual this Akran Súr. I have met him frequently at the royal palace of Elén. I have always thought him as a charming Erkún, and remarkably intelligent. His success is all the more surprising, taking into account that he is a low-born," said King Frederick.

"I indeed do concur, your Majesty. He is quite an extraordinary figure, albeit ambiguous in his intentions. Nevertheless, I must concede that his mediations have generally been successful," explained King Robert.

"Be mindful of the Erkúns, your Majesties. They are sly creatures, who can never be fully trusted. Also, from what I have heard, this Underworld dweller is particularly persuasive," warned Múzlak.

"There is no harm in dealing with both magical races, dear Kaldára. It has always been so since the Peace of the Tiba was enforced, and to the great benefit of all. Nevertheless, there is some truth in what you say. My spies in Sarandos tell me of the proximity of the Ambassador to the new King of Karlún: a young and ineffectual fool. He will not last long among those rebellious generals and nobles. Their loathing for that family runs deep. That being said, who knows what words the Erkún and the young King are exchanging," said King Frederick.

"Perhaps it is my order's inherent distrust of the Underworld races, but I would now advise you not to receive the Ambassador for the time being until further notice," advised Múzlak.

"A rather rash recommendation, if I may say so, Múzlak," replied King Robert in a baffled manner.

"There is something quite not right here, your majesties. I can sense it. Something stirs under the surface of the earth. A dormant malice which may be re-awakened sooner rather than later, wittingly or unwittingly," lamented Múzlak.

"That is a rather sombre reflection, dear Kaldára. I am not sure whether there is evidence to justify such terrible foreboding. The problems which we face now are habitual, hardly a prelude to an apocalypse," said King Frederick in disbelief.

"Mark my words, your Majesties. Something odious conspires against the order of the world. I only wish my suspicions are proved to be false. That is why I beseech you both to keep your armies on the highest alert possible, in order to face the potential nightmare that awaits us," said Múzlak sternly.

"A little exaggerated, I must say. Nevertheless, it is better to be safe than sorry. Your advice shall be followed in Thámrod," said King Frederick.

"It shall also be followed in Skrallog, young Múzlak. Let us pray that your misgivings are nothing more than that," said King Robert.

As the hours of light finally came to an end, so did the conversation between the two monarchs and the Kaldára. While it had a more or less productive encounter, it had ended on a somewhat awkward note. Both Kings looked at Múzlak with a hint of derision, even if they did not express it with words, in the interest of courtesy. His words of warning seemed bizarre to them to say the least. Yet, he could not let such suspicions lie. Over the coming months he would need to get the bottom of the matter as soon as possible. However, if his instincts were proven to be correct, then he would not have to long to wait.

Chapter 6

An army for a soul

A full moon shone in the night sky over the lands west of Karlún, perfectly illuminating all things which lingered on the surface of the world. The stars were numerous in number and added a further sense of beauty and tranquillity to the rarity that is a night with full moon. Such a pleasant view of the night sky however, did not exactly comfort King Julius and his army of ten thousand armed, torch bearing Snails marching under the banner of their realm.

The harsh volcanic lands west of Karlún are troublesome enough to cross in daylight. Travelling through them under cover of darkness is even more problematic for even the sturdiest of creatures. Indeed, Insects particularly feared moving out in the open in all the lands (even those astride steeds such as Woodlice, as was the case of Julius and his nobles), due to the grave dangers posed by larger creatures who feasted on the flesh of Insects, such as Birds or Bats.

Nevertheless, the young monarch did not allow himself to be overcome by uncertainty or fear. For Akran Súr had assured him that no beast would bestow harm upon either himself or his army. Yet, the Erkún had conveyed this message to the King not in person, but in his dreams. The first dream was ignored by Julius, as it could have merely been a coincidence that he had dreamed of the Erkún. However, when the dream recurred for over a week, repeating the same message over and over again, he suspected that the Ambassador of the Underworld was genuinely speaking to him.

In this strangest of dreams, Akran Súr instructed Julius to mobilise his army and to march westwards to meet the Council of Erkúns outside the Gala Gún, to await further negotiations and that the road to the door of the Underworld would be safe, as the Erkúns controlled the beasts in the area. For four days, the army of Karlún had marched, without a single incident involving attacks by animals. The fact that such assurances turned out to be true, made Julius both respect, and fear the Erkúns and their power.

While King Julius was vaguely enthusiastic about this meeting with the powers which ruled the Underworld, others within his camp were not so keen on this adventure. The most prominent of these sceptics being a substantial percentage of the Karlúnian nobility accompanying him, and his very own mentor, Severus.

"I must be frank, Your Majesty. I do not feel at ease with the road we are taking at this moment in time," explained Severus.

"Then, what is it in particular that troubles you about this whole affair, Severus?" asked Julius, visibly irritated by the sincerity of his mentor's remarks.

"It is the whole nature of this deal which disturbs me, Sire. It doesn't make any sense. Why on earth, would the Erkúns be willing to offer their armies to aid one realm? It has never been done before in the history of Insectdom. I fear a darker motive lies behind the seductive words of that accursed Ambassador. As the old saying goes, never trust an Erkún," said Severus.

"Please, enough of the foreboding, Severus! I have been hearing nothing but grief from you ever since we crossed the Anozáth. Why must there always be a conspiracy by all and against all? Is it not possible that this is a genuine offer of alliance and friendship, between two races that have been downtrodden and exploited by those around them? In any case, the mistrust of our people towards Erkúns may have only been a spell cast on us by the Kaldáre, in order to strengthen their hold over us. Everyone has interests, even those who openly espouse selflessness, Severus," replied Julius in a slightly angry tone.

"It was not my intention to question your judgement, Sire. I am merely stating my own personal misgivings on the matter. You have always appreciated my frankness on such issues," said the monk, trying to control his temper.

"Indeed I have always done so. Yet, now is the time that I need your counsel and support more than ever. I cannot afford to look weak and isolated in front my people, especially the nobility and the army. That is why this negotiation must go well. If they do, then perhaps my position as King will be secured. Remember that, my dear Severus," whispered the young King, so as not to be heard by those behind them.

"As you wish, Sire," replied Severus reluctantly.

However, judging by the morale of the Karlúnian host marching towards the Gala Gún, it could be said that the young monarch's paranoia was not totally unfounded. The soldiers and nobles marching under his banner generally looked discontented and ill at ease at having to march during the night. With no visible enemy with whom to fight, the whole escapade seemed to them to be little more than the whim of an adolescent minded monarch.

Yet, even if morale had been high among the ranks, it would be to no avail. This was not the mighty, well equipped Karlúnian army which swept all before it in the days of old. Indeed, the general malaise which infected the realm had also spread to its soldiers, making them resemble little more than an armed rabble, which was unified solely by the hatred felt towards Thámrod. As a result, loyalty towards the monarch of Karlún, was now hanging by a thread.

It was almost dawn, when the host of Karlún finally reached the outer ring of the rocky labyrinth which concealed the Gala Gún. King Julius ordered his troops to stop marching and to await further instructions. He had no intention whatsoever of taking his soldiers and nobles into that vast, impenetrable maze. Akran Súr had told them merely to wait outside the labyrinth, and that was where they would remain.

"Where are these accursed Erkúns? What kind of hosts keeps their guests waiting for over an hour?" retorted the Duke of Sarandos: one of the nobles in the King's entourage.

"They shall reveal themselves soon enough. I am sure of that, your Grace. All that is needed is a little patience," replied King Julius looking over at his nobles.

Suddenly, the sound of beating wings could be heard from a distance in the dark. It was coming from the maze itself, and it was getting louder and louder. Whatever was in the air was slowly gliding towards the Karlúnian army and it was heavy, and it was not alone. The noise made by these mysterious beasts greatly unnerved many of the Snail soldiers, who in turn drew their weapons, waiting nervously for their potential assailant. Yet, all of a sudden, the sound of beating wings began to slowly die. Whatever had flown out of the maze had now landed outside it, and proceeded to advance towards the Karlúnian army on foot, and it sounded very heavy indeed.

In response to such menacing sounds, King Julius had ordered his troops to get into defensive positions, waiting for their potential assailants to reveal themselves. Only once they stepped into the torchlight, would the King's archers be allowed to open fire. Suddenly, a booming voice could be heard coming from the dark. As menacing as it sounded, hearing it brought relief to Julius. He knew perfectly well whose voice it was: that of Akran Súr.

"Be not afraid, my friend. We are the Council of Erkúns, seeking to parlay with Your Majesty. We do not wish to bestow harm upon you," said the Ambassador in a reassuring tone.

"Good evening, Ambassador. It is a great pleasure to hear you once more. Please, step into the light," replied Julius.

Slowly but surely, the Erkúns began to reveal themselves to the Karlúnian host. Out of the shadows emerged the six imposing members of the Council of Erkúns, whose very appearance inspired a certain degree of unease and fear among the ranks of Snails present. At the head of these mighty creatures, stood Akran Súr and Hordar, ready to exchange words with their guests.

"Your Majesty, allow me to present to you, his Excellency Hordar the second: Emperor of the Underworld," said Akran Súr, presenting his superior with one of his mighty limbs.

"It is a great pleasure to finally meet you, your Excellency," said Julius, bowing respectfully, as did his fellow Snails.

"The feeling is mutual, Your Majesty. The Ambassador has spoken very highly of you. I wanted to see for myself, whether his words were well founded," explained Hordar.

"The Ambassador is far too complimentary your Excellency. I am merely a young Snail with much to learn still," replied Julius humbly.

"A young Snail you may be, but from what I have heard and what I sense in you, you have a tremendous potential yet to be unlocked," said Hordar.

"Thank you, your Excellency," responded Julius politely.

"The Ambassador has spoken to me at great length about the troubles your realm is currently suffering. I cannot help but feel sympathy for your people. We also know what it is to feel downtrodden and scorned by those who believe themselves to be more powerful," said Hordar.

"Indeed, that is so. However, the Ambassador informed me that your Council wishes to make me an offer which would be greatly beneficial for my realm. That is why I am here," said Julius in a more serious tone.

"Of course, your Majesty. Taking into account the predicament of your realm, and the needs of the Underworld, the offer I am about to give you, may shock you in its generosity. As it is quite clear that Karlún is incapable of paying its debts, I am willing to offer an alternative arrangement to the one which is currently in place," explained Hordar.

"I am listening," replied Julius inquisitively.

"My people have grown weary of the darkness of the Underworld, and the injustices imposed upon us by the Kaldáre: a fate similar to yours in your relations with Thámrod. Therefore, I will give the order for my armies to leave the Underworld. They will assist you in crushing your enemies, whoever they may be. Once your foes have been reduced to shadows and dust, I shall make you Viceroy of the East. All the lands between the northern coastline of Skrallog and the southern shores of Gorgán shall be yours and yours only. I demand only two things from you in return," explained Hordar.

The scale of the offer left many of the Snails present both confused and breathless, none more so, than the King and his entourage. Just exactly why would the Erkúns be willing to concede such a tremendous asset to the realm of Karlún?

"The offer is indeed incredible, your Excellency. I still have trouble believing in its authenticity. What exactly do you require of me, in order to receive such a handsome reward?" asked Julius, visibly perplexed.

The Emperor of the Underworld took a step forward to place his enormous left limb on the young Snail's right shoulder, and his leaned his head forward, proceeding to whisper in his ear.

"Your absolute loyalty, and your soul," snarled Hordar in a slightly menacing manner.

"I beg your pardon?" retorted a startled Julius.

"You will rule as Viceroy of the East in the manner that may please you, while my people shall have the remaining lands of Insectdom carved up between them. Nevertheless, you will answer to me. You shall obey me at all times, and never question any commands that I may give you. The power of the Erkúns is limitless, and the path to immortality will be open to you. Give me your soul, and you shall live forever," said Hordar, while his fellow Erkún grinned gleefully.

King Julius could not believe what he was hearing. The reward was far greater than anything he could have ever imagined. Accepting it would make him the greatest ruler Karlún had ever seen. Finally, he would be able to prove his worth to those who had doubted and scorned him. Yet, a terrible doubt clouded his mind.

The cost of such incredible power would come at a potentially terrible price.

"Your offer has left me speechless, your Excellency. I do not know what to say," said Julius, as confused as ever.

"I must protest, Your Majesty. You must not accept this offer. The cost is far too high for it to be worth the reward. Think of your own soul and of the realm, sire!" interjected Severus, his abrupt remark visibly irritating the Erkún present.

"Be silent, Severus! Your interruptions will not avail me!" barked Julius in response.

"These creatures are treacherous! They cannot be trusted whatsoever. There must be another way to save our realm, sire!" cried Severus, glancing nervously at the Erkún.

"Enough of this charade!" growled Akran Súr, who turned his gaze towards Severus. In a split second the monk was levitated several feet off the ground, grasping at his throat. The hapless Snail was being choked by a ring of fire.

"No, wait! Do not harm him!" cried Julius, while his soldiers drew and aimed their weapons at the Erkún.

"Kneel before your Emperor, or the monk dies," snarled the Ambassador.

In turn, the young monarch did not hesitate in kneeling before his new master, and in return Akran Súr dropped Severus to the ground. He did his utmost to hold back the tears, but to no avail. Hordar now towered over him, once again placing an imposing limb on him.

"You have chosen wisely, your Majesty. You must now fulfil one final task before our new alliance can be forged. Rise, Viceroy," said Hordar.

"What is it you ask of me, your Excellency?" asked a tearful Julius.

"You must first destroy your closest enemies: those that do not trust you, those who deceive you, and those who wish to see your head on a spike," snarled Hordar, whose words were followed by the sudden levitation of Severus, and all of the Karlúnian nobles and generals present, all of them being strangled by fiery rings.

"These treacherous beings have been conspiring to overthrow you the minute the crown of Karlún was placed on your head. How can such wretched creatures be loyal to their Viceroy, and to their Emperor? Traitors must be punished in the manner which they deserve," ordered Hordar, glancing over at the hapless Snails.

"It's not true! The Erkún is lying! Do not listen to him!" cried Severus in desperation.

"There is no conspiracy, sire! The Erkún is playing with your mind!" screamed the Duke of Sarandos.

"They are lying, Viceroy. You may not sense it, but I can. I can feel their treachery, and it is a strong emotion indeed. Draw your sword and execute every single one of these foul Insects! Show them no mercy!" barked Hordar.

Julius drew his sword and stood before his new victims. Yet he could not bring himself to cut them down in such a pitiless fashion. He was no tyrant. He was not his father.

"Why do you delay, Viceroy? Kill them now or all shall die, both those present and all the realm of Karlún. Ending the lives of these twenty two Insects, is the only way to save your realm," snarled the Southern clan leader.

One by one, the twenty two Insects condemned to die were beheaded by the tearful monarch, who at least managed to dispatch them with swift, clean strokes of his sword. His dear friend Severus was the last to perish. The blank expression of his mentor as the royal blade was brought down on his neck would haunt Julius until the end of his days.

The carnage left many of the Karlúnian soldiers perplexed and shocked. They could not believe they had witnessed. No monarch had ever executed every single noble in his realm, and certainly not all at once in full view of his soldiers. A cold, dull sense of fear now gripped the Karlúnian host: a fear of their King. This, was exactly what the gleeful Erkún, had wanted.

"You have acted justly, Viceroy. These creatures desired nothing but misfortune for you. Now, you can be the ruler you were born to be," said Hordar reassuringly, putting his limbs on the Julius' shoulders.

"I am your humble servant and I will do as you command, your Excellency. But I beseech you! Please do not make me slay any more of my own people," mumbled Julius.

"Indeed, I shall not. It will now be your foreign foes, which shall now feel your wrath," said Hordar.

"It is now settled then. Now come the days of alliance between the realm of Karlún and the Underworld. May the Gods bless them now and forever more!" cried Akran Súr. In turn all the Erkúns present roared in unison, startling the Snails.

The Emperor of the Underworld now turned to face the Ambassador and gave him the following instructions in Erkún tongue.

"Return to the Gala Gún, summon the twelve hordes," growled Hordar.

"With pleasure, your Excellency," replied Akran Súr.

Soaring high into the sky, the Ambassador set his course for the maze where the dreaded door of the Underworld lay concealed.

Upon arriving at this accursed gate, the Erkún positioned himself on the edge, looking down at the bottomless pit beneath him. Slowly, he pulled out a mysterious looking object from within his purple robes: a small, silver horn adorned with the black skull of an Erkún: the Horn of War as it was known in the Underworld. He then proceeded to bring it close to his imposing jaws and blew on it.

The noise emitted from this disturbing looking horn was almost deafening. It could be heard for miles around, and forced Julius and his troops to cover their heads in agony, completely unused to such noise. Thrice, did the Erkún blow the horn, and thrice did the Snails writhe in terrible discomfort. An eerie silence then descended upon the lands around the Gala Gún. However, that peace would soon be broken, by the sound of something far more sinister.

A distant rumbling could now be heard rising from the depths of the Underworld. The ground itself began to shake. Something was moving below the Karlúnian host, and it was advancing towards the surface. It was some time, before King Julius and his troops could see movement on the surface. A distant glow of flaming torches could be seen slowly advancing through the maze, accompanied by blood curdling cries which sent shivers down the backs of those Snails present. A monstrous host was making its way to the exit of the rocky maze.

"Behold the twelve hordes of the Underworld! We now march to war! The East will fall! To war, my children!" bellowed the Emperor.

The young King of Karlún looked on in awe at the power on display before him. As far as the eye could rank upon rank of heavily armed Ants were marching in unison, flowing out of the darkness of the Underworld: Ants are physically intimidating Insects to many. While not being particularly tall or large, they made up for their lack of height with their deceptively phenomenal strength. Their multiple limbs had the strength to break the necks of far larger beasts and they could carry objects many times heavier than their own bodies.

But it was their black, lifeless eyes and their great pincers that disturbed other Insects. For it demonstrated their unnatural nature, a form of life more suited to the dark depths of the Underworld from whence they came. Their dark red armour, long pikes and mighty shields, served to intimidate their foes even more. Yet, these foul creatures were not to be the only to serve the Erkúns and Julius in this war. A loud buzzing noise could also be heard from within the maze.

Out of this impassable labyrinth emerged another terrible host. However, this horde was airborne: swarms and swarms of Wasps. If the Ants were intimidating troops, the Wasps of the Underworld were the shock units of the Erkún's armies. Almost twice as big as an Ant, the typical Wasp was a formidable warrior. Wearing a suit of armour of the same black and yellow colours as their skin, they were very hard to slay, not least because they were very skilled at fighting with long swords with their multiple limbs. Their speed and mobility in their air also made them lethal archers: a constant threat to all those unable to take to the skies to fight them. Among these elite warriors, the most dreaded were the Hornets: beasts far larger than the typical Wasp and wielding frighteningly large axes.

Julius continued to look back on in awe at what he saw marching behind him. Any lingering feeling of guilt which he felt for things passed, was replaced by his all-consuming ambition. For the first time in the history of Insectdom, a surface Insect was to lead the terrible hordes of the Underworld. The power which was now in the limbs of the young monarch was far greater than anything he could have ever imagined. Finally, he would be able to restore his realm to its former glory, nay surpass it. Whether he would be able to control these dark forces at his disposal would be another matter entirely.

Chapter 7

Treachery in the Mountains

I t was a gloomy early evening, when Lazimóff reached the edge of the grim, forbidding peaks known as the Dead Mountains, after having managed to pass through the extensive blockade set up by the besieging army of Moriátin. When it came to the names of natural wonders, many were rather undeserving, either being exaggerated or underwhelming in nature.

However, in this particular case, the mortals who first came up with such a title were absolutely right in their assertions. For the mountains looked very dead indeed, and had done for quite some time. While imposing in stature, the mountain range was as lifeless as the surface of the Moon. Nothing more than barren, razor-sharp rocks with naught but the most miserable lichen as food for those beings desperate enough to live in such a terrible place.

The gloomy light and the persistent drizzle only enhanced the bleak appearance of the mountains. Nevertheless, Lazimóff knew that he could not let it affect him in any way possible. His mission remained the same. He sought an audience with the Butterflies of these parts, and no bad weather was to prevent that from coming to pass.

Slowly but surely, the young Kaldára ventured on the dark pathways which cut across the mountains, not fully sure of what awaited him within the murky nooks and crannies. Lazimóff crept along the lifeless paths up into the peaks. Ever so slowly, did the Bumble Bee rise higher and higher.

Despite a considerable sense of fatigue, Lazimóff persevered and did not let his body get the better of him. After having reached a height of several thousand Insect feet, the Kaldára broadened his mind, to sense what was around him. Just as he had foreseen, he was not alone among the jagged rocks.

While he couldn't physically see any creatures around him, he could however, sense them perfectly. So confident he was in his own power, that he even contemplated whether the Insects who wished to ambush him were even aware that their actions and intentions were known in advance by their supposedly ignorant target.

As soon as darkness fell fully over the land like a sombre shroud, Lazimóff brandished his staff, producing a red light from the ruby at its tip, using it as a torch. Barely a moment passed, when the expected ambush commenced. From all sides, around three dozen Insects leapt out of their hiding places, and unleashing a devastating volley of poisoned tipped arrows at their victim. A mere mortal would not have withstood such a ferocious assault.

However, Lazimóff was no normal creature, for he had foreseen the barrage in slow motion merely moments before it came. As a result, not a single arrow successfully struck him. They had all rebounded off a great red-coloured force field which had sprung up over the Kaldára and his woodlouse, flowing out of his staff, and which protected him fully from any physical damage from any mortal weapon.

While the assailants continued to fire volley upon volley at him, Lazimóff could take a clear look at who was foolish enough to assault him. He soon realised that his aggressors were Butterflies: local residents of the Dead Mountains. At long last, the Kaldára had come across the very beings with whom he sought to parlay in the name of peace.

"Cease in your hostilities towards me! I do not come to bestow harm upon you fine fellows or any of your kin. I come with tidings to your realm, and with counsel," said Lazimóff in an authoritative manner.

"Who dares to walk into our home unannounced, like some malevolent thief?" barked the commanding officer of the ambush party.

"It is I, Lazimóff the Kaldára: successor to Báldur as envoy of peace among the Insects of the south. I come to parlay with your rulers, to discuss the possibility of peace terms with your brethren of Moriátin. They will know that I speak the truth," explained Lazimóff assertively.

"Wait here, until we confirmation of this, sir," replied the commanding officer.

———◆≈◆———

After almost an hour of delay, messengers reached the party of soldiers to confirm that the Kaldára was indeed expected. With identities confirmed, the commanding officer and his troops (much to their embarrassment) escorted the Bumble Bee to the main settlement of the Butterflies which lay concealed within the deepest circle of peaks within the mountains.

If the scenery on his visit to the Dead Mountains had been rather disappointing for the Kaldára, then his dissatisfaction was not to come to an end when coming across what passed for civilisation among these foul, lifeless rocks. The place which many of these Butterflies called home was austere in the extreme. Here there was no beauty, no sophistication, nor finesse. Here there was just the bare minimum to survive in the grim wasteland. The dwellings were built of stone, with a rudimentary design that suited the terrain to perfection. In such a harsh landscape, practicality and not luxury, was the key to survival.

Indeed, even the house of the most powerful noble was rather sombre. Its furniture was grim and exuded a melancholy and depression which Lazimóff had not yet felt on his travels. The leading aristocrat whom the Kaldára had come to meet was a certain Count William of Nárim. Although it had been many centuries since the Butterflies had driven out of their ancestral home in the lush forests of Nárim by the Moths, this noble family still kept the name of the woodland realm in the title. Perhaps as a souvenir of a happier time: a time which was now long gone.

The aristocrat himself was not a particularly cheerful creature. He was of median stature and rather slim, concealed under battered old brown robes. The extensive wrinkles on his face and limbs suggested a Butterfly of advanced age. Yet, when the Count spoke, he oozed intellect and exuded a fiery determination.

"So, the snobs of Moriátin are so incapable of negotiating, that they send a Kaldára to do it for them? Hardly the most surprising thing I've seen from them. I was half expecting you to be an assassin," sneered the Count.

"I do not come in the name of Moriátin, but in the name of peace, good sir. Believe me, if I had come to slay you, then you would already be dead," replied Lazimóff cheekily.

"That is what they always say, and yet I still find it hard to believe. You are not the first sorcerer with whom I have crossed words," said Count William coldly.

"None like me, however. That I can assure you," responded Lazimóff defiantly.

"I shall be the judge of that. So, what it is this grand new plan that you come to propose to me, that is so different from others I have heard before? Does Queen Alessandra wish me to kiss her ring as well as kneel before her and beg for mercy?" asked the Count sarcastically.

"Such mortal trivialities are of no concern to me, Count. My proposal is simple: you both end hostilities immediately and you shall be granted safe passage to negotiate a settlement in Nalgála," said Lazimóff.

"Your predecessor suggested something similar some years ago. Do you see us at peace now? How can there possibly be peace with a people who have shown us nothing but contempt ever since the act of union between our two realms. The insufferable arrogance, the loathing of our culture and our language has done nought but increase over the years. I myself and others before me fought for the armies of Moriátin with courage and distinction in its wars against the Bees of Anóg, and that is how they have always thanked us. Never in my whole life, have I heard a word of gratitude from the snobs of the north. There is only so much a proud people can take. We shall rid ourselves of the tyranny of Nalgála, sooner or later," growled the Count, stroking the arms of his throne.

"Unlike my predecessor, sir, I do not come here to beg you to stay in the union. Instead, I would argue for the independence of your people, albeit in a peaceful and orderly fashion," explained

Lazimóff, trying desperately to be as diplomatic as possible to his cold, hostile host.

The Count's face changed expression abruptly. He could not believe his senses that a Kaldára was actually in favour of his cause. Could it be true, or was it a mere ruse to deceive him?

"Your words surprise me, Kaldára. I did not expect an establishment figure to side with my people. Yet, how can I be sure that your words are sincere. After all, you're not the first magical creature to endorse our cause. The Ambassador of the Underworld also expressed support not but one year ago," said Count William in a slightly more friendly tone.

"Unlike the Erkúns, I do not have selfish ulterior motives. My priority on this earth is peace, and not its territorial boundaries," said Lazimóff sternly.

"So, you would grant me safe passage to Nalgála?" asked the Count, visibly more interested in his unexpected guest.

"Indeed, I would, sir. I will even escort you, so as to guarantee your safety. I must be frank. Negotiation is your only hope of success. Militarily, your cause is doomed. You're besieged and outnumbered, and the chances of victory against the superior forces of Moriátin are slim. Please, do not let your people perish in a futile act of self-immolation," said Lazimóff.

"You underestimate our resolve, Kaldára. However, I will heed to your advice, albeit with great reluctance. So what is to be done?" said Count William.

"Tomorrow at dawn, we shall head northwards, where we shall meet my fellow Kaldára Grizwald at the Bridge of Elubí. I shall put forth my case to him, and then we will all continue northwards to Nalgála, where peace terms shall be agreed. Once that is done, you will be allowed to return home. Nothing more, nothing less," explained Lazimóff.

"What if your fellow sorcerer does not concur with your line of thought?" asked the Count sternly.

"He will agree, of that is no doubt. Trust me, good sir," replied Lazimóff cockily.

"For your own sake, I hope you are right," said Count William.

It was almost eleven o'clock at night, when Lazimóff finally went to bed, in the guest quarters of the Count's mansion. As he slowly tried to get to sleep, he reflected on the issues discussed earlier on the evening. For the first time on his travels, he had dealt with the unusual experience of dealing with creatures which were not overly sympathetic to his presence. Perhaps the Kaldáre overestimated their importance and prestige among lesser mortals, or perhaps the Erkúns had poisoned their minds? Whatever it was, Lazimóff did not feel entirely at ease with what had come to pass.

Perhaps he had been too rash in his remarks on the break-up of Moriátin. After all, he wasn't even sure if his fellow Kaldára would agree to it, least of all the rulers in Nalgála. Nevertheless, they were hardly spoilt for choice in terms of finding solutions to this bitter conflict. With those doubts lingering in his mind, the young Kaldára dozed off to sleep, shortly to be consumed by his dreams.

Several hours passed, and much to his discomfort, Lazimóff was not having the most pleasant of nights. His visions were troubling and at times terrifying, for he saw many terrible things happening in his subconscious. He could see multiple monarchs, nobles and military commanders all across the world, being assailed and slain in their very beds by mysterious assassins: killers of dark origins and intent. Some such as Queen Alessandra of Moriátin were fortunate enough to escape death, but others were not so lucky. Indeed, those that survived were in the minority. Even his fellow Kaldáre were being assailed, even if they did escape the fate of so many others.

Suddenly, Lazimóff woke up abruptly from his slumber and in great apprehension. He realised that what he was seeing were not premonitions of future events, but visions of current ones. The Insects he saw were actually being physically attacked and murdered in real time. The assassinations were authentic, and seemingly carried out in a co-ordinated fashion by unknown beings. But who and why, he asked?

However, something stopped him abruptly from reflecting effectively on the matter. Several drops of liquid were falling from the ceiling and landing on his head. Much to his disgust, what fell on him was blood: Butterfly blood. The moment the Kaldára looked up, he saw trouble. Two large Insects dropped from the ceiling and only the Bumble Bee's lightening quick reflexes saved him from being skewered by their blades, and who instead managed only to impale his bed. Only when on their feet did both the assailants and their target see each other under the moonlight.

Before Lazimóff, stood two large creatures entirely coated in imposing suits of armour and armed with long swords of finely crafted steel and large, unwieldy maces. Their heads were also obscured by reinforced helmets, with only two parts of their bodies being visible to the naked eye: their wings and a bright green flame under their visors. In simultaneous fashion they brandished their swords and pointed them at the Kaldára. In a flash two bolts of lightning shot out of the blades and straight towards Lazimóff, who managed to dodge them once more thanks to his reflexes.

Facing formidable opponents of magical power, the Bumble Bee summoned his staff with his mind and engaged his opponents toe to toe. For almost ten minutes the three magical beings exchanged blows and bolts, until at last Lazimóff managed to defeat his foes, leaving their corpses as little more than piles of ash.

With his assailants vanquished, the Kaldára looked closer at the Insects who had sought to slay him. Indeed, he soon came to realise that these were no normal assassins of this world, but Demons of a terrible power. No other creature could possess the form of an Insect, yet possess a naked skull for a head. Only by looking at their shrivelled helmets, could he deduce their origins: four golden stars adorned imprinted on the perfectly forged steel.

In was in that moment, that all became terribly clear to him. The beasts were members of the Blood Brotherhood: a fraternity of powerful Demon warriors, who answered to only to the Erkúns. The fact that their deadliest servants had sought to kill him, could only mean that their orders came from their fearsome masters themselves.

However, Lazimóff had been so consumed by his own peril that it took a few moments more to realise that he was not the only one to have been targeted. Multiple screams echoed across the Dead Mountains. Lazimóff could not let panic spread like the wildfire it could so easily become. He had to see whether his visions had indeed come to pass.

As the young Kaldára hurried through the halls of Count William's residence, he discovered much to his horror, the aftermath of what had taken place. The hysterical cries of several servants led Lazimóff to the quarters of Count William. After having temporarily consoled them he looked upon who had until some hours ago been his host. Now, he looked on at the lifeless corpses of both Count William and his wife impaled to their beds with long daggers driven through their necks, their bed sheets drenched in their own blood.

Fearful that the killers could still be in the vicinity, Lazimóff brandished his staff and urged the servants to get down. After careful inspection, he saw that the coast was clear and there was nothing to fear, for Lazimóff looked on from the balcony and saw two other terrible assassins flying away off into the distance. Their task had been done.

It was only after an hour of closer inspection and investigation that the victims could deduce exactly the damage done to them. The Demons of the Underworld had successfully assassinated all the most important leaders of the rebellion, save one general who had escaped a similar fate thanks to being in his mistresses' residence and not his own. His wife however, was not so lucky.

Alas, the Kaldára sensed that the aftermath was the same across multiple realms, from north to south, from east to west. Indeed, there were few crumbs of comfort for him to savour, among which he could count the survival of the Kaldáre and a mere handful of nobles and the occasional monarch.

The nature and organisation of this plot both impressed and disturbed the young Bumble Bee greatly. They had known exactly when and how to weaken the realms of Insectdom. By slaying the elites of each race, they had neutralised their capacity to act quickly and effectively in the face of aggression. The sheer efficiency of the operation, gave the impression that it had been planned far in advance by a cunning mind. Immediately, Lazimóff suspected who had planned this: the only Erkún who had personal contacts with so many of the most important figures throughout Insectdom, Akran Súr.

Only such a mischievous and devious creature such as the Ambassador could have devised such a plot over time, having been so frequently among the rich and powerful of earthly society. The sense of shock within Lazimóff had now been replaced by a feeling of uncontrollable outrage.

After centuries of hard-earned peace, the Erkúns had broken their promise to withhold the Peace of the Tiba. Their treachery was now laid bare for all to see. The brutal murder of the ruling classes of Insectdom, was only the beginning. War was now upon the earth once more. Now, only the Gods would know who would be the victors, and who would be the vanquished.

Chapter 8

The Sack of Hakím

The south eastern roads of Insectdom are arduous ones for those who wish to take it. While the risk of being devoured by ravenous beasts was considerably lower than in other parts of the world, they were not without their peril. The arid landscape is almost permanently exposed to the fierce glow of the Sun, and only spared during the hours of darkness. The horrifically high temperatures during the day and the almost sub-zero ones during the night, made meticulous preparation for such a voyage an issue of paramount importance. This was all the more important, when it involved moving entire armies across the endless sand dunes.

It was the newly proclaimed Viceroy of the East who now led vast hosts across the barren desert. So enormous was this army, that from the sky it could be seen marching across the dunes for several Insect miles. Yet the hordes which he commanded were quite unlike any other that had come before. Never in the history of Insectdom, had a ruler from the surface commanded both troops from his or her realm, and the foul beasts which dwelled among the fires of the Underworld.

The demoralised Snails of Karlún for the first time in their history, now marched shoulder to shoulder with rank upon rank of fearsome Ants, and protected in the air by a tremendous swarm of Wasps, Hornets and dozens of gigantic Erkúns and Demons circling above. Thanks to his terrible pact with the rulers of the Underworld, the hapless Snail now had the power to strike and seize whatever he pleased.

While his first instinct was to wheel his mighty hordes northwards towards the hated realm of Thámrod, he was advised against it by the Erkúns. Indeed, they argued that it would be more prudent for them to head south to strike at another target in order to protect the soft underbelly that was the south of Karlún. The realm which would be the first to feel this terrible wrath would be the Kingdom of Gagorland. With more than three thousand years of history as a united political entity, the Maggots had long been a major oriental power, with a very distinctive culture and had frequently jostled with Karlún for supremacy of the lands to the south east.

The jewel of this proud, ancient realm was its capital city: Hakím. It was concealed within the very depths of the desert and lying on top of the largest natural well in the world, and was structured upon multiple levels, meaning that any potential invader would have to work his way down in order to control the city fully. The imposing sand -coloured walls adorned with razor sharp thorns, made the settlement was almost impregnable and as a result had rarely fallen to foreign foes in all its history of existence. Yet, history would now count for nothing. As mighty as Hakím was a city, it had not faced the wrath of hordes such as those of the Underworld for a very long time.

Under the scorching midday sun, Julius dismounted from his steed, visibly uncomfortable in his heavy suit of plated armour. He looked on at the imposing fortress city that lay before his troops.

Although his vast host was well equipped for the attack against Hakím, Julius very much doubted the possibility of capturing it swiftly. In his opinion, it did not matter how many battering rams, siege towers or trebuchets his troops had at their disposal. He had read enough military history to know the defensive strength of the Maggot capital. Many a Karlúnian army had been laid to waste trying to capture it, and there was no guarantee that Julius' host would not face a similar fate.

There was also the issue of the lack of surprise. The great horde under his command had been unable to advance as swiftly as expected, due to the need to deal with the powerful border forts which the Maggots had across their frontiers. The fact that some of the enemy's soldiers had managed to escape the initial onslaught, meant that the capital was well-informed of the force which would come to besiege it, and would in turn double its efforts to prevent the foul spawn of the Underworld from breaching its solitary black, iron gate.

"There is much conflict in you, Viceroy. Why are you so troubled?" inquired Hordar, landing beside the young Snail, flanked by Akran Súr.

"I very much doubt the possibility of a swift victory, your Excellency. Many an army has failed to breach the walls of Hakím. This city is more than prepared to withstand a long siege," replied Julius.

"Your concerns are well founded, if one refers only to the battles of the past. But this is a new era, Viceroy. The filth that lies behind those walls has no living memory of the power of the Underworld," snarled Akran Súr.

"The Ambassador is right. We cannot let the past cloud our current judgement. I recommend that you command your troops to encircle the city immediately, lest the Maggots wish to escape," said Hordar.

"The issue is not the siege itself, your Excellency. Even if the city's defences are destroyed, it is almost impossible to break the gate down from the outside. It is forged from black iron, and can withstand any force that is thrown against it," explained Julius.

"Fear not, Viceroy. That is a minor issue that shall be dealt with swiftly. Now, we must prepare for battle," said Hordar in a reassuring tone.

With a swipe of one of his mighty limbs, the Emperor of the Underworld ordered his minions to prepare for the task that lay ahead. Once again, the deafening Horn of War sounded across the land, to the great discomfort of those terrestrial beings unaccustomed to such wretched noise. The vast hordes now began to set in motion. The Snails of Karlún began to organize themselves into a defensive position, directly facing the gate of Hakím, just out of range of the trebuchets which dotted the Maggots' mighty walls. Meanwhile, the Ant columns began to spread out, flanking the Snails and enveloping the city, leaving it completely encircled. There would be no escape now, for those that lay behind the walls.

The first terrible wave of attack would come from the Erkúns themselves. Under the leadership of the Emperor himself, these formidable beasts took to the skies and glided effortlessly towards the walls of Hakím. The response of the defenders was swift and fierce, unleashing a terrible barrage of arrows and stones against their assailants. However, much to the horror of the defenders, this onslaught had little or no effect on the attackers. After all, Erkún hide is incredibly thick and can withstand any earthly impact.

Having withstood the defensive storm, the Erkúns now proceeded to launch their own, terrible power on the hapless Maggots manning the walls. One after the other, the dreaded sorcerers of the Underworld unleashed volley upon volley of Erkún fire: flames so powerful and all-consuming that even stone itself burned. Within a matter of minutes, the fire laid waste to the defences upon the walls, melting the fixed fortifications and obliterating the wretched Maggots which manned their positions, many falling to their deaths writhing in agony at being consumed by the ferocious flames.

With the upper defences destroyed, the Ants and the Snails began to advance towards the walls, while the Erkúns began to bombard the interior of the city, supported by swarms of Wasps and Hornets who landed on the walls and began to fight their way downwards, clearing out the lower defences which were still manned by the Maggots. While the city continued to receive barrage after barrage from the multiple trebuchets manned by the Ants and the Snails, thousands of the foul creatures of the Underworld began to scamper up the fortified walls, completely indifferent to the storm of arrows and spears which inflicted substantial casualties upon their ranks.

Meanwhile, Julius ordered his own troops to continue advancing towards the gate itself, placing his large battering rams at the front of the assault. Concealed under iron shields, the hundred or so Snails operating each of the battering rams were vulnerable only to enemy fire on their flanks: something which in the current context of the battle was unlikely. In spite of desperate resistance, the Snails reached the gate, and soon began to pound away against the mighty iron structure, while their infantry proceeded to erect planks to slither up the walls to eliminate the defenders.

Time after time, the rams struck the gate with their powerful steel heads, yet it still held firm, seemingly unaffected by the onslaught.

———◆⊰◆———

After several hours of fruitless attacks, the tide began to change. Something strange was happening within the walls of Hakím. Much to the surprise of Julius and his company, the gate of the city began to slowly open. This unusual action was indeed puzzling for the Snails. Were the Maggots opening the gate to surrender? Or had the Erkúns managed to unlock it from the inside? Whatever it was, all would be revealed soon enough.

Once the gates had finally swung open, the assailants could look upon the terrible destruction they had unleashed upon the Maggots. The city was almost totally concealed in a shroud of fire, ash and smoke, thereby reducing visibility to a considerable degree. The only distinguishable shapes which could be seen clearly, were the Erkúns circling above. However, the city had not fallen yet, despite its desolation. The blast of a battle horn and cries of rage could be heard from behind the fumes, and soon the ground began to tremble. Unsure as to what foe would emerge, Julius beckoned his troops to take positions and stand fast, bows at the ready and pikes lowered.

What emerged from the darkness, were Maggot soldiers in tightly organised fighting columns. Concealed under their suits of grey armour, broad shields and long spears, they resembled an armoured tortoise: almost impossible to break through. However, it was not the armoured infantry columns which most intimidated the foes of the Maggots. Indeed, the real strike weapon of the desert realm, were the beasts they used in battle.

Between the multiple columns, scampered gigantic Scorpions as black as the night sky and tall as a small house, and ridden by three Maggots (one to control it, the other two as archers). Indeed, many a foe had suffered the devastating inflicted by the mighty pincers and stings of these imposing creatures.

Despite the formidable appearance of the Maggot host, it was clear that the attack was little more than a final stand. With nowhere to run, the Maggots had decided to participate in one final act of gallant self-immolation. As soon as the desperate defenders reached their assailants they were met by showers of Snail arrows and pikes and from devastating volleys of Erkún fires.

So terrible was the Snails' defence, that the Maggot counterattack was broken within a matter of minutes. Only some of the Scorpions had managed to break through the ranks, inflicting substantial losses before finally being subdued. With organised resistance now effectively broken, the path to securing Hakím was now fully open to the invaders. Nothing now stood in the way of Julius from taking the city.

It was at the crack of dawn, when the city finally fell to the ravenous hordes which had besieged it. An eerie silence now fell upon the battlefield: a calm which was broken only by the occasional bloodthirsty cries of victorious Ants and the buzzing of Wasps flying overhead. The once proud city of Hakím had been reduced to little more than rubble after the siege. Barely a single building had survived the onslaught intact.

The stench of burnt flesh was so overpowering that it was nauseating. Indeed, it was difficult to see anything of substance from afar, due to the rising smoke. Many of the inhabitants had either perished or fled via the underground tunnels which connected the wells. Those fortunate enough to have survived were confined to the city centre, under the watchful gaze of the soldiers of Karlún.

Overseeing this terrible carnage was Julius, now looking on from the main balcony of the city's royal palace. Located on one of the central levels of the city and protruding over the central well, the home of the now late King of Gagorland was unusual in its design. A small pyramid of brown stone to onlookers from the outside, but which concealed a stunning maize of rooms richly adorned with multi-coloured mosaics, and culminating in a beautiful sapphire coloured fountain in the centre of the building. The very fact that Julius was the first monarch to capture Hakím in over two thousand years was a source of immense pride. If only Julius' ancestors could look upon him now as the master of this mighty city.

Yet, the Snail was not alone in his admiration for his achievement. Down from the skies descended the two main architects of his great achievement. Both Hordar and Akran Súr wished to join the young Viceroy to revel in their great conquest.

"You have proved your valour in battle, Viceroy. You have broken a great realm, and it shall not be the last," Hordar said triumphantly.

"There is no one of high birth left to organise resistance against us, Your Excellency," said Julius.

"Alas, there is always someone left who is willing to fight, Viceroy," warned Akran Súr.

"That is indeed true, Ambassador. Never underestimate the will of those who refuse to see the end of their rule, Viceroy. The love of power and gold within the nobility is far stronger than the affection they may hold for their dearest. You all of people, should know that, Sire," said Hordar.

"What now then?" asked Julius.

"The city is now yours! Henceforth, Hakím is now part of the realm of Karlún. Its inhabitants will swear an oath of loyalty to you in exchange for their lives to be saved, and you shall rule them as you see fit. Once Gagorland is fully subdued, you can return to Sarandos as a victorious conqueror, and the people will love for you it, and will yearn for such glory to continue forever more" explained Hordar.

"A great prize this is indeed. Alas, at this moment in time, I am too weary from battle to be able to scheme to the best of my abilities. I must recover my strength as soon as possible," replied Julius, visibly fatigued from the exertions of combat.

"A quite understandable position indeed, Sire. Go now and rest. But we cannot linger for very long. Within the next few days we must push on eastwards towards the city of Ashúr. If that mighty port falls, then all of Gagorland will be yours," said Akran Súr.

With that, Julius proceeded to slither off the balcony towards the door, in search of a warm bed in which to sleep. To his surprise however, the door was not open to him. Hordar had positioned himself directly in front of it, completely blocking the Snail's access.

"If it's not too much trouble, I would like to go to sleep, Your Excellency. Could you possibly move away from the door?" asked Julius, slightly confused.

"Oh I could, but I'd rather not," replied the Emperor, with a dubious grin.

"We have just realised that there are matters of pressing urgency, that still need to be discussed," explained Akran Súr, who in turn had positioned himself behind the Snail, and placing his limbs over his shoulders.

Having two very large Erkúns in such close proximity made Julius very uneasy. Both smiled mischievously and it disturbed him greatly. What on earth were they doing?

Suddenly, a terrible thought crossed his mind. For the first time since being named Viceroy, Julius suspected that he was being betrayed. Before he could draw his sword to defend himself, Akran Súr grabbed the Snail by the throat. The crushing power of the Erkún left Julius motionless, unable even to attempt to break the stranglehold. Slowly, the Ambassador of the Underworld lumbered towards the balcony, lifting the Viceroy up into the air over the great drop over the city's gigantic well.

"You promised me power, Ambassador. Now you betray me," whimpered Julius, barely able to speak.

The Erkún brought the Snail closer to his face, the stench of ash overwhelming the hapless monarch.

"I have a terrible little secret to tell you. I lied, as I have from the very beginning. You should have listened to your pitiful monk when you had the chance. Did you really expect us to allow you to rule in our name? The Underworld and the surface realms cannot co-exist and they never will. You have been deceived," growled Akran Súr, his yellow eyes fixed upon the startled Snail, while the Emperor cackled evilly.

"Be done with him, Ambassador," growled Hordar in Erkún Tongue.

"I bid you a fond farewell, Viceroy," whispered Akran Súr before hurtling Julius off the balcony. Like a stone the young monarch plummeted to his death, and who in his final moments was too weak even to scream. The rule of King Julius of Karlún had ended the same way with which it had started: with a whimper.

"I actually pity the poor devil. He actually thought we were sincere in our wishes to help him," said Hordar disbelievingly, while watching Julius fall.

"Desperation and a lust for power are a dangerous combination, Your Excellency. It is amazing to see how blind lesser beings become, once consumed by those emotions," replied Akran Súr.

"Indeed, it is. It is most pleasant to see that our armies have not faltered in their duty," remarked Hordar.

"Of course, Sire! This is just the beginning. Once the east falls, so will the rest," said Akran Súr, overlooking the carnage they had brought upon the Maggots.

"The very thought of such an outcome, brings me great pleasure. Nevertheless, despite our overwhelming strength we must act with restraint. Our troops must only act bestially with those willing to resist. We cannot risk creating new potential rebels to our rule," explained Hordar.

"I couldn't agree more. However, there is also the issue of land distribution. All of our kin must have the right to possess lands throughout Insectdom, no matter their caste," responded Akran Súr.

"You were always the idealist, my friend. Alas, I very much doubt the Clan leaders will take too kindly to the idea of plebs owning lands," said Hordar.

"With so much land potentially at our disposal, I am sure they will come to accept it in time," said Akran Súr.

"That may all be well and good, Akran Súr. But we cannot allow ourselves to become distracted from the task at hand. A war has begun, and we must strive to end it on our terms as soon as possible," said Hordar.

"Indeed, we do. Nevertheless, there is still the issue of the Kaldáre that needs to be resolved. I sense that the Blood Brotherhood has failed in its attempts to slay them," warned Akran Súr.

"Alas, I felt it too. Perhaps we have underestimated their power, after all. Yet, the deaths of so many monarchs and nobles throughout Insectdom, will have weakened their resolve in any case," replied Hordar reassuringly.

"Yet, they still remain a threat. I will hunt them down personally and destroy them," growled Akran Súr.

"Your resolve is admirable, my friend. I, on the other hand, must continue fighting the war. Perhaps it will be best to divide our forces. Six of our Ant Queens must take their hordes westwards. I shall continue with the others to proceed with the taking of our next great prize: the port city of Ashúr. With Hakím in ruins, I very much doubt they will put up resistance. Especially if we offer them generous terms to serve under us," explained Hordar.

"Your wish is my command, Your Excellency," replied Akran Súr.

With those words, both Erkúns took off from the balcony and set off on their respective missions. Both had very clear ideas on the tasks that lay ahead of them. The conquest of Insectdom would be arduous and difficult to achieve. Nevertheless, the Erkúns were confident in victory. After all, they were numerous in number and powerful by nature. Their hordes were unmatched in their ferocity in battle, and few armies in the world would be able to withstand them.

The sack of Hakím was just a taster of what was to come. Those that co-operated with the Erkúns would be spared in exchange for submitting to their rule. Those that refused or resisted, would meet a similar fate to those wretched Maggots who had dared to stand up to the might of the Underworld. The revenge of the Erkúns was now in motion, and war was now upon Insectdom. How and when this terrible conflict would end, would not be clear to even the wisest of mortal beings. Only the Gods would now know the fate which would await the peoples of Insectdom, for better or for worse.

Chapter 9

A Time of Great Peril

Time is a curious phenomenon to those fortunate enough to be aware of its existence. In times of joy and of plenty, it is a swift companion which leaves mortal beings looking back in amazement on how fast it moves during their lifetimes. However, in times of great darkness and misery, then it becomes a cruel burden upon the hapless, dragging on without an end in sight.

The latter was the de-facto feeling among creatures north of the River Tiba. Two years had passed since the brutal sacking of the city of Hakím. A great many events had transpired following that cataclysmic atrocity. The armies of the Underworld had succeeded in overrunning the all of the realms south of the River Tiba. City after city of Snails, Spiders, Moths and Maggots and Butterflies burned in the fires of the Erkúns. Those that surrendered managed to survive thanks to accepting a servile form of collaboration with their new masters. Many thousands more of these unfortunate Insects fled northwards, in a desperate attempt to escape the terrible wrath of the invaders.

One such gathering of refugees was located not far from the banks of the River Tiba, next to the mighty Bridge of Elubí. As far as the eye could see, countless half- starved Insects congregated in small groups next to makeshift tents in miserable conditions. The rains came again, as they did every autumn, and as usual they transformed the lands below them into a wretched quagmire of stinking mud. Such dreadful conditions, only further exacerbated the feeling of hopelessness and despair in the encampments along the river.

Among these hapless creatures, were the three Kaldáre of Insectdom, Queen Alessandra of Moriátin and a few more nobles her and there, and those of other races. The assassination attempts perpetrated by the Blood Brotherhood had taken a severe toll on the elites of all the realms of Insectdom. Indeed, in the case of the Butterflies, less than ten percent of the original nobility and military leadership still survived. Most were congregated close to their Queen and the Kaldára next to a large fire concealed under a large white tent, looking on at the many more thousands of helpless Insects crossing the mighty Bridge of Elubí.

Despite the feebleness of the refugees, they were not totally without protection. On the northern bank of the river, an extensive network of trenches, thorns and multiple other defensive works had been constructed around the bridgehead, guarded by thousands of hungry and soaked Insects concealed under armour and water proof cloaks, looking on apprehensively at the endless columns of civilians crossing the bridge, half expecting a surprise assault to occur at any moment.

"The rains are heavy this autumn. A bad omen this is, I fear," muttered Queen Alessandra, looking on at the multitudes still pouring into the gigantic encampment from the marginal comfort of the royal tent. Fully dressed in a suit of splendid silver coloured armour, the Butterfly had to be ready for battle at a moment's notice. After all, the enemy was swift and unpredictable, capable of striking at will with amazing speed.

"The omens are bad regardless of the weather, your Majesty. At present, it is not the rains that I fear the most," the Duke of Elénluin wearily.

"With such a pessimistic outlook, the enemy already has won the battle before it has already begun!" grunted Múzlak judgementally.

"My fellow Kaldára is right. As perilous as our predicament may seem, one must always trust a hope," said Grizwald in a reassuring tone.

"Alas, the events of the last two years have caused me to take such a view, Grizwald. It is difficult to retain much hope, when the cities of half the world lie in ashes and in the hands of the hordes of the Underworld," replied Alessandra sternly.

"Nevertheless, we must maintain our composure in the face of this adversity. The enemy must be stopped before he completes his task," interjected Lazimóff, trying to establish a measure of coherence to the discussion at hand.

"A feat easier said than done, Kaldára. Have you seen the vast armies the Erkúns have mustered across the River Tiba?" said the Duke of Elénluin with a hint of sarcasm.

"That is why a strong defence of the bridges across the Tiba is of paramount importance. If we stop the hordes of the Underworld there, then the chance to turn the tide will perhaps arise," replied Grizwald, gazing sternly at the Duke.

"Yet, we should not merely contain ourselves to holding the bridges, Grizwald. A great deal more aggression is needed in our strategy. A strong and decisive counter stroke is what's needed at this moment in time," said Lazimóff.

"With what troops, master Kaldára? We do not have the numbers for such a grand offensive!" replied the Duke sharply.

"If we merely hold our ground on the bridges, we shall be overrun with ease! That is why I would propose to send another force across the river and attack our enemies from the rear!" explained Lazimóff.

"Alas, my dear old friend, even if that were so, we are not fully aware of what the enemy has in terms of strength beyond the river. The power of the Erkúns is clouding our vision," said Grizwald glumly.

"Grizwald is right, Lazimóff. We cannot risk the lives of thousands on such a reckless adventure. After all, should we fail, the poor civilians around us who remain will be at the full mercy of the hordes of the Underworld," interrupted Múzlak.

"It seems then, that our list of options grows thin. We have no choice but to hold the bridges, and pray to the Gods that our defence is strong enough to stem the enemy's advance," said Queen Alessandra.

"There is, one other possibility, Sires," said Múzlak.

"Yes?" asked the Duke inquisitively.

"We seek the counsel and the aid of our brethren across the Northern Sea. I will personally volunteer to gather what support I can," explained the Dragonfly.

"You are aware of the laws of the Kaldáre, the laws of our ancestors. If you return to the Lost Island before your time in Insectdom is done, then your life will be forfeit. Condemned to suffer punishment for your failure," warned Grizwald.

"I have no other choice, my dear old friend. It is I who must do it. Alas, I do not possess the same warrior spirit that you and Lazimóff have in abundance. If by some miracle, I am to convince our brothers and sisters to come to our aid, then it will not have been in vain. If my life is to be forfeit, then so be it," said Múzlak calmly.

"Your words are noble, Múzlak. Yet, I do not understand why you must bear such a burden. Allow us to come with you," said Lazimóff.

"No, Lazimóff. I will not let your names be besmirched by my actions. Better to lose only one Kaldára, then three. Besides, your wisdom is needed here, my friends. My mind is made up, and I shall leave at nightfall," replied Múzlak.

"So it is settled, then. We are now all aware of the task at hand," said Queen Alessandra to all her fellow colleagues, who nodded in unison.

Night fell upon the encampments around the northern banks of the River Tiba, and mercifully the rains had temporarily ceased. Nevertheless, the end of the storm did not signal an end to activity on the surface. Múzlak had already set off northwards, meanwhile Lazimóff was heading to organise the defences to the east, at the Bridges of Asor and Algas.

As for Grizwald, he would be the sole Kaldára who would remain at the helm of the defences of the west, providing whatever counsel he could to the Insects before him. Heaven knows, that the wretched beings needed it. It would require all of his power (and indeed luck) to help stem the dark tide that was upon them. Indeed, it was the fear of this great peril that kept the Insects working on strengthening their defences.

In their desperation, the Butterfly nobles had decided that their own professional soldiers would man the most forward defensive positions facing the Bridge of Elubí, while every able bodied adult refugee would man the rear fortifications. Due to the fact that most of these peasants, craftsmen or physicians had never even held a sword, they were being given an intensive course in basic combat. Queen Alessandra was perfectly aware that their military value was next to nothing. She only prayed that the hordes of the Underworld did not break through the professional ranks of the defenders. For the poor civilians would be slaughtered with relative ease.

It was around one o'clock in the morning, when the Butterfly sentries saw movement coming across the bridge, in the form of a glimmering light from a torch. Before they could raise their bows to fire at the oncoming Insects, a loud horn sounded across the fortifications: the horn of Moriátin.

"The scouts have returned! Hold your fire!" exclaimed one of the senior sentries.

After having flown over their fellow soldiers, the scouts proceeded to head towards the royal tent.

"Your Majesty, our scouts from across the river have returned and they seek an audience with you," explained one the royal guards, while his colleagues kept the visitors waiting.

"Send them in, forthwith!" said Alessandra sternly.

The scout party which entered the royal tent was a sorry sight indeed. Three Butterflies stood before their Queen and nobles and Grizwald. Their cloaks and armour were battered, and their faces bearing scars of battle.

"Your Majesty, I bring grave news from across the river," said the senior scout, with a bandage across his right eye.

"What is it?" asked the Queen apprehensively.

"A mighty horde has reached the southern bank of the Bridge of Elubí. Even as we speak, thousands upon thousands of Ants, and Wasps are crossing the river, protected in the sky by dozens of Erkúns and members of the Blood Brotherhood," explained the scout glumly.

"What of the rest of your party, soldier?" asked the Duke.

"My three other soldiers were slaughtered in an ambush by Wasps. We were fortunate enough to escape with our lives," said one of the other scouts, consumed by exhaustion and fear.

"There is no time, Sire. The enemy host will reach us within one day. Battle is upon us," warned the senior scout.

"So be it. To your positions everyone! Be ready for battle within a day!" said the Queen defiantly.

"As you wish, your Majesty," replied all those present in the tent, who then set off swiftly to their respective posts.

Speed was now essential. There was now no more time to build new defences. All they could now do was wait patiently for the menace that would soon come.

In a show of bravado, Grizwald positioned himself at the very front of the defences, joining the soldiers in the closest trench facing the Bridge of Elubí. Being unable to see the enemy with the naked eye, the Kaldára decided to leap out of the trench (much to the bewilderment of the Insects around him) and sit himself cross legged directly in front of the bridgehead.

With his body in position, the Praying Mantis sat up, closed his large eyes, and sunk into a deep meditation. Every ounce of his strength would now be dedicated to the psychological voyage that awaited him. Magical meditation was a power that very few creatures on Insectdom possessed, and the Kaldáre were among the minority which could wield it. Those fortunate enough to be blessed with such abilities could transport their minds to the far corners of the globe to see what lay ahead, and to even read the thoughts of lesser beings.

In the blink of an eye, the Kaldára's subconscious transported itself across the River Tiba to see what dreaded foes marshalled before the hapless Insects of the north. Indeed, Grizwald did not like what he saw at all. As far as the eye could see, rank upon rank of heavily armed Ants marching in perfect unison, the sound of cumbersome armour crashing down on the Bridge almost deafening, and their path perfectly illuminated by the thousands of torches which they bore. These foul creatures also moved with them hundreds of siege weapons which were perfect for use against the major northern cities, with the most imposing of these being gigantic trebuchets.

Above the dark hosts glided ever more menacing beasts than them. Thousands of Wasps and Hornets had also been called to lay waste to the north. Yet above all else, it was the dozens of Erkúns and their Blood Brotherhood which troubled Grizwald the most. Wary of the fearsome power which the lords of the Underworld possessed, he focused his meditation on them, trying to see in their minds, their thoughts and their ambitions.

Suddenly however, the Kaldára felt a sharp pain in his head. At first he believed that it was nothing more than a temporary headache. But almost instantly he deduced the origin of this discomfort. Someone else was also meditating, and it was not a Kaldára.

Perched upon the edge of the bridge in a similar trance, was Akran Súr: Ambassador of the Underworld. The Erkúns did not move or speak as a normal being would, and instead began to converse with Grizwald telepathically.

"I can feel your presence, Kaldára," snarled the Erkún in the mind of the Praying Mantis.

"The feeling is mutual, Ambassador," replied Grizwald.

"Your efforts are in vain, good sir. No amount of meditation and foresight will aid you now. Didn't your predecessors tell you that my people also possess such power?" said Akran Súr mockingly.

"Your heartless ambition seems to know no bounds, Ambassador. My predecessors should have warned me of the danger that you possessed to this world," said Grizwald sternly.

"Indeed, they should have done so, Grizwald. However, as powerful as they were, they were always blind to my real intentions. Such was the effectiveness of my false charm and affability, their contemptible snobbery and blind obedience to the laws of your order that they could not even see through the false persona which I held for over a hundred years," explained Akran Súr.

"I should have guessed that an Erkún was not to be treated with. Faithless and accursed creatures you have always been, and will continue being so until the end of your days. So contemptible is your race, that your master does not even grace us with his presence," said Grizwald.

"Even in adversity you are as self-righteous as ever, Kaldára. Nevertheless, you are probably right in that respect. The Kaldáre and Erkúns can never truly co-exist in peace, even if we are more similar than you think: a fact that makes it all the more tragic. Oh indeed, what a brilliant alliance we could have forged!" said the Erkún, his voice as imposing as ever.

"We are nothing alike, Erkún," replied Grizwald angrily.

"Oh but we are, Grizwald. We are. Both our races possess rare gifts of terrible power. Both of us are aware of the pathetic weakness and corruption of the Insects and seek to control them as best we can," said Akran Súr.

"My order only seeks to keep the peace among the peoples of Insectdom. Do not compare the noble mantle of my forebears with your squalid, underhanded scheming!" replied Grizwald, barely containing his rage.

The Erkún in turned laughed loudly at the words he had just heard.

"You do indeed amuse me, Kaldára. Even now you still believe the nonsense they told you back on your island. So consumed by your pomposity and smugness you all are, that you remain unaware to the fact that your desire to control the filthy creatures of this world is as strong as ours! Deep down, we both know that the peoples of Insectdom cannot be left to their own devices. They are so blinded by greed and corruption and their lust for war, that there is no choice but for us to control them. Sooner or later, you will come to that realisation, whether you like it or not," snarled Akran Súr.

"It is none of our concern how the Insects conduct themselves. Our mantle is to merely prevent them from destroying their world and nothing more. Your ambition will soon be your downfall, Ambassador. You will never rule Insectdom, and you will never wrest the crown of the Underworld from your master, no matter how powerful you may think you are," said Grizwald defiantly.

"You underestimate me, Kaldára. Day by day, I grow stronger and stronger. Once the lands of the north have been razed to the ground, I shall slay the Emperor and take the crown for myself. Indeed, so powerful am I, that I care little if he senses our conversation right now," said Akran Súr menacingly.

"Be careful what you wish for. Never must you underestimate the fear of death. It can be a powerful asset in battle. You have deprived your slave races of emotion and that it precisely the weakness which they possess," said Grizwald.

"Do you still seriously believe that your pathetic rabble can withstand the might of the armies of the Underworld? Your cause is lost, Grizwald. The peace of the Tiba shall be cast into the flames and you shall personally witness the total failure of your order. Then, once my task is complete, I shall tear you apart limb from limb," growled Akran Súr.

"The dark shadow which your race has cast upon this world will soon be gone. I look forward to personally striking you down on the battle field tomorrow," said Grizwald, with a hint of malice in his voice.

"Insolent, Kaldára! I shall enjoy slaying you, and tossing your severed head into the Tiba!" boomed the Erkún.

Within a flash, the meditational period of both creatures ceased, and they returned to the world of the living. As with any period of telepathic conversation, the immediate after effect was one of considerable dizziness. Indeed, so dazed was Grizwald, that he almost fell to one side. However, he managed to maintain his balance and slowly come to his senses.

The power of the Ambassador had left Grizwald slightly shaken. Perhaps the Erkún was right after all? Perhaps both races were not so different from one another? Was Insectdom so decadent and rotten, that it was now beyond saving? Nevertheless, even if there were a vague validity to the arguments, the Kaldára could not allow himself to be seduced by them. Instead, he had to use his advantage the one weakness that the Erkúns possessed: overconfidence. With enough preparation and enough courage maybe, just maybe, the dark tide could be turned. Only the Gods would now know the fate of Insectdom: a fate which would now be decided at the banks of the River Tiba.

Chapter 10

The Bridgehead

The Gods were not merciful on the defenders of the Bridge of Elubí. The arrival of the early morning sun was blocked by yet more torrential rain. If fighting a bloodthirsty horde was difficult enough, doing so in such wretched conditions was even worse. Yet, the Insects manning the defences did not complain. The thousands of Butterflies, Slugs from the Valley of the Leaves, Moths from Nárim, and numerous other races merely stood and waited for the onslaught that was upon them. For the first time now, the enemy was in full view. The foul cries of the ravenous Ants could be heard, sending shivers down the backs of the inexperienced peasants manning the rear areas.

Directly facing the horde of the Underworld stood Grizwald, Queen Alessandra, her uncle and the smattering of surviving nobles of all the races. In a brave gesture of defiance, the Queen of Moriátin lifted herself out of the trench and drew her long, elegant sword and brandished it at the enemy host.

"Brothers and sisters, our time of suffering ends today! Today, the differences between our races do not matter! Today, we face a common enemy, and a wretched one at that: a foe that despises us for wanting to be free. The slaves of the Erkúns shall pass no further! Today they shall meet their end here, at the Bridge of Elubí! Show this Underworld filth no mercy! For you shall receive none in return! Make those you hold dear proud of you today, in victory or in death! Stand fast, and do not falter!" bellowed the Queen defiantly, who received a booming battle cry from the thousands of Insects behind her.

The noise which followed this gesture however, was far more imposing. The horn of the Underworld blared out across the trenches, leaving its defenders clasping their heads in terrible agony.

Moments later, the dark horde fired its multiple trebuchets and catapults, launching a shower of great boulders. Three waves of this terrible onslaught struck the trenches, demolishing several dozen towers, slaying and wounding hundreds. Following the siege weapon attack, the sky turned as black as the night itself with three devastating volleys of arrows which blocked out the light. They too, made their mark despite desperate attempts to avoid them. Many were the Insects writing in agony with an arrow or two protruding from their bodies. Despite these terrible onslaughts and the potential outbreak of panic by the untrained peasants at the rear, the defenders stood their ground.

The first wave of enemy attackers which came in to swoop on the multi-racial ranks were the Blood Brotherhood, swords and axes brandished and ready to unleash the full fury of the Underworld upon them. This time however, the onslaught would not succeed. Grizwald leapt out of the trench and raised his staff above his head. In a split second a searing bolt of light shot up into the sky, and transformed itself into a gigantic green dome which shielded the Insects below from attacks from above. Time after time, the Demons tried to break through the shield with their lightning bolts, yet to no avail.

So ineffective was the Demons' assault that their masters swooped in to aid them. At first the sight of the Erkúns terrified the Insects below, yet their initial fear subsided when they saw that even the fire of these mighty beasts could not pierce Grizwald's mighty shield.

Nevertheless, the enemy was cunning and as the Erkúns circled above the first wave of Ants charged towards the trenches. The foul creatures found to their great surprise that the bridgehead was far more heavily defended than originally anticipated. Without the power of Erkúns fire to clear the path, the Ants found considerably difficult to work their way through the gigantic thorns, spikes and other multiple defensive works in place. Those that managed to get past these obstacles and within striking distance of the trenches, were cut down by a devastating volley of Butterfly arrows.

Much to the ferocious rage of the Erkúns, the first wave was totally destroyed, with not a single Ant having managed to strike his foe with his weapon. The relative ease in which the onslaught had been repulsed had surprised many of the defending Insects. However, that sense of false security soon dissipated when faced with the following waves.

Again and again, rank upon rank of Ants crashed against the trenches, suffering appalling casualties. Oblivious to the losses being suffered on the ground, the six Ant Queens decided that the best way for their armies to break through the defences was through sheer brute force and attrition: a tactic which was deemed inevitable due to the inability of the Erkúns to attack effectively from above.

Slowly but surely, the Ants cleared their path by setting fire to the defensive obstacles which prevented them from using their overwhelming numbers. After several hours of intense battle, the bridgehead's obstacles had been destroyed, and the road to the trenches was now open. After having repulsed around a dozen waves of Ants, the first line of defence remained intact and had suffered minimal casualties. Yet, its troops were exhausted and in dire need of replacement.

However, before that essential reinforcement could be carried out, the tired Butterfly, Moth, Maggot and Snail soldiers found themselves facing the most ferocious onslaught so far. Scurrying towards them at great speed over the mountains of Ant corpses were hundreds of gigantic, filthy brown Rats, each with two Ants astride them: one controlling the beast and the other as an archer. Though many of these repugnant beasts were felled by arrows and spears, a great many more managed to break through and inflicted considerable casualties on the front line, ripping many an Insect to shreds with their jaws while their masters shot others with arrows.

As with all other previous assault, the main focus of their attack was the central position occupied by Queen Alessandra, Grizwald and the nobles, yet to no avail. Indeed, the Butterfly monarch acquitted herself well in the skirmishes, felling many a foul beast with her long, elegant blade in a bid to protect the Kaldára.

After facing several waves of this devastating form of cavalry attack supported by many more Ants, the defenders sensed the hopelessness of their position and consequently fell back to the next defensive line. Their retreat was in turn harried from above by arrows being fired by Wasps. Yet again, the defenders were offered no respite. The second defensive position soon found itself under attack from the Blood Brotherhood and thousands of Wasps and Hornets who landed in the trenches, using their hand to hand fighting skills to slaughter countless defenders.

After another hour of fierce fighting, it was terribly clear that the second defensive line would also fall within a matter of minutes. The Erkúns had ceased in their attempts to attack from above, and had now landed and fighting on the ground, inflicting devastating casualties on their foes. In the chaos of battle, Grizwald took the Queen to one side.

"Your Majesty, our positions will not hold much longer. Make your way with haste with your uncle to the rear and organise the counter-attack. I will stay here and hold them off as long as I can!" cried Grizwald over the deafening noise of steel and flesh clashing incessantly.

"I shall! Do us proud, Kaldára," replied Alessandra, with a hint of mischief in her eye.

"Have faith, your Majesty," said Grizwald, who looked on briefly as the Queen and her entourage pulled back to the rear.

If the hordes of Ants and Wasps had proved to considerable foes in battle, they were nothing in comparison to what was in store. By early afternoon, the second defensive line had fallen and the surviving defenders had pulled back to the third position. This was the last stronghold held by professional soldiers. If they fell, behind them were the two remaining defensive lines held by untrained peasants. This meant that the third line had to hold at all costs.

In turn, the Erkúns now focused all their efforts on finding Grizwald and to slay the troublesome Kaldára once and for all. Swatting aside any Insect that stood in their way, three Erkúns lunged furiously at the Praying Mantis. After a lengthy confrontation involving the use of magic and fire, Grizwald managed to slay his three terrible opponents. Alas, they would not be the last. Yet there was a small sliver fortune about slaying the mighty beasts. When an Erkún died, so did the demon which guarded it.

By mid- afternoon, the third defensive line was about to fall. Its defenders had been decimated, and were now close to retreating, despite Grizwald's best efforts to rally them. Even if the Kaldára had managed to lay waste to almost a dozen Erkúns, the hordes of the Underworld were an endless tide. It was now only a matter of time, before the bridgehead would collapse and fall completely into the hands of the enemy.

Faced with seemingly hopeless odds, the survivors from the third defensive line fell back, unable to withstand the limitless minions of the Underworld. Now, all hope would rest on the shoulders of the stout-hearted, yet hopelessly untrained peasants manning the rear. How long they would be able to stand their ground, was something unknown to all but the very Gods themselves.

However, before the ravenous horde could fully unleash its bloodthirsty fury upon the battered defenders of the bridgehead, it was stopped in its tracks by the sound of the arrival of new participants to the battle. Another horn sounded across the wreckage of the battlefield. This time, it belonged to no spawn of the Underworld, but the kingdom of Moriátin.

On both sides of the disputed bridgehead, two large formations of thousands of Insects astride proud and sturdy Woodlice, (with the Queen Alessandra at the head) emerged from over the hills and set upon their foes in a mighty cavalry charge that was a sight to behold. Despite their best efforts to stop the onslaught dead in its tracks with barrage upon barrage of arrows, the Ants and Wasps could not prevent the determined attackers from ploughing straight through the Underworld's ranks, and relieving the exhausted defenders. Despite the initial success of the charge, the attack was not without casualties, the most important one being the Duke of Elenluin, who was felled by four Ant arrows while he charged through enemy ranks.

With a new enemy to face, the Erkúns ordered their minions to focus their efforts on the new opponents and to ignore the hapless peasants. All followed this order, except one. There was one creature who would not be parted from his personal mission, and that was Akran Súr. Oblivious to the new orders from his superiors, he paid no attention to the new assailants and advanced towards Grizwald himself, with his loyal servant the Dead Knight at his side.

Seeing the furious Erkún lumbering towards him, the Kaldára leapt out of the trench to protect his fellow Insects and to deal with this troublesome diplomat.

"Your plan has failed, Ambassador! Perhaps it is time to reconsider!" cried Grizwald with a hint of mischief, with the obvious intent of provoking his opponent.

"Enough talk, you sanctimonious fool!" growled Akran Súr, launching a terrible volley of fire from his mouth in the direction of the Kaldára.

In turn, the Praying Mantis blocked the flames with his staff and returned the volley to its master. Simultaneously, the Dead Knight came to his master's aid launching multiple lightning bolts at the Kaldára. Time after time, the three magical beings attacked, blocked and parried each other, seemingly unable to make a breakthrough.

Enraged at the inability of his servant to strike a blow, the Erkún raised a mighty hand and struck the Dead Knight with such a terrible force, that the Demon was physically removed from the ground and sent rocketing into the sky into the clouds, never to be seen again.

Now only the Kaldára and the Erkún stood face to face. Both on the verge of total exhaustion, they knew that there was now only time to land one final blow. Whoever did so, would be the victor. In an act of sheer desperation, Akran Súr raised his limbs, levitated two Ants and one Moth battling nearby and hurled the hapless Insects towards the Praying Mantis.

Grizwald managed to lift his staff in time to stop the Insects from crashing into him. Nevertheless, he was unaware that just as the Ants and Moth were cast aside, the Erkún himself had followed them closely behind, swiftly leaping up and striking the Kaldára with his powerful right hand, sending both the sorcerer and the staff flying.

Dazed and bruised did Grizwald land in the muddy quagmire that was the battlefield. As he opened his eyes to look where he was, he could see the Erkún hurtling towards him at great speed from above. The Ambassador of the Underworld now towered over him, and unleashed one final volley of terrible fire.

Yet, the flames never reached the body of the Kaldára, for he stuck out his own right limb to block the fiery volley, and much to the surprise of the Erkún, hurled it back at his assailant. Grizwald howled in agony as his right limb was reduced to a blackened, shrivelled stump. However, his opponent was in visibly more dire straits.

Akran Súr lay writhing on the ground, totally consumed by his own flames, screaming at the top of his lungs, as his body was slowly being burned to a crisp. With every passing moment, the Erkún became more and more physically incapacitated, unable to move or respond to anything around him. Therefore, Grizwald took the opportunity to summon his staff, and launch one final green bolt which struck Akran Súr squarely in the face, and consumed his entire body in an emerald light, until there was no physical remain. The Ambassador of the Underworld was no more.

Grizwald collapsed onto the earth in total exhaustion, barely conscious of the great feat he had achieved. He had almost single handed defeated more than a dozen Erkún and servants, decimating the leadership of the Underworld's ranks. As for the battle raging around him, he could sense that the tide had turned and it was coming to an end.

Slowly but surely, the defenders of the bridgehead were driving back what remained of the ravenous horde. By that evening, the battle was over. Four out six Ant Queens had been slain, and the remnants of their armies had either been driven onto the bridge or into the river to drown. Only the Wasps and Hornets chose to fight and die where they stood, and not a single one survived.

The sense of relief and joy could be felt all across the battlefield by the surviving combatants. From the highest born noble or monarch, to the most humble peasant, there was recognition of the enormity of their achievement. For the first time in several years, the armies of the Underworld had been stopped dead in their tracks. Their great victory would forever be remembered in folklore as the Battle of the Bridge of Elubí, and would serve as a great inspiration to all those resisting the Erkúns.

The feeling of jubilation was soon replaced however, by exhaustion and repulse. For the lands on which they currently stood, were a filthy, wretched quagmire of blood and death. The putrid smell of thousands upon thousands of slowly rotting corpses consumed the air, making it very difficult to breathe.

Gradually, the survivors began piling up the bodies of the deceased and burning them on hastily set up pyres. At this moment in time, there was no time for concern about who lay on them. In the interest of the most basic hygiene, Ant, Butterfly, Wasp, Moth and others, burned together.

It was not until nightfall itself that an exhausted Queen Alessandra and her greatly reduced entourage of nobles and generals came across Grizwald. Indeed, they found the tired sorcerer sitting upon a small rock, looking on at the multiple pyres and the flames which were now lighting up the night sky.

"Your optimism was well founded, Grizwald," smiled Alessandra.

"Perhaps it was, indeed. Yet, our victory has come at a most terrible price," replied Grizwald.

"Alas, victory seldom comes without great carnage and suffering. Our realms will grieve greatly tonight," said Alessandra.

"At least, the enemy has been stopped. The peoples of Insectdom are as not as weak as he once supposed," said Grizwald with a hint of optimism.

"Indeed, that is so. What has become of the Erkúns leading the filthy hordes?" asked Alessandra.

"All dead, all rotten," replied Grizwald sternly.

"As it should be, then I presume. However, what is to be done now, I wonder?" asked Alessandra.

"For now, we rest. After that, we must gather our strength and come to the aid of those in need to the east," said Grizwald.

After all, the Kaldára was not mistaken in his assessment. The battle in the west may have ended favourably. But, the war was not yet won. For the Erkúns still posed a threat to other parts of Insectdom. Any gain here at the Bridge of Elubí, could soon be wiped out by a catastrophic defeat in the lands to the east. Aiding Lazimóff was now Grizwald's task at hand, no matter the peril.

Chapter 11

A sight for sore eyes

Surrounded by woodland, Lake Birthas stood between the Valley of Leaves to the West, and the Spider realm to the east. Yet while one could expect such a place to be a pleasant retreat from civilisation, they could not be further from the truth.

Lake Birthas was a cold, lifeless place. The woodlands surrounding the lake were dead, and had been for some time. No animals grazed here and the trees and plants were a lifeless grey, their leaves long since gone. Passers-by had always wondered what had killed the woodland. Was it some natural infection, or was it something else that had provoked the decay, something far more sinister. As for the lake itself, it too was as lifeless as a corpse. No fish dwelled in the cold murky waters of the lake and it had been the case for centuries.

The horrendous autumn weather and the ever closer cold of the upcoming winter made any sojourn here, all the more unpleasant. Yet, for the first time in many a decade, the lifeless woodlands were hosts to a great number of creatures. Many thousands of Snails, Bees (from the great woodlands of Anóg), Spiders, Maggots and Flies shivered under whatever refuge they could find. A great number of them were soldiers, battered and bruised in their armour and holding their blunt weapons. However, they were but a small minority in comparison to the number of civilian refugees who dwelled reluctantly in these parts.

The reason for the presence of so many wretched Insects in one of the most unpleasant locations of the world was one of necessity and not of choice. The scourge of war had brought them here, and they had nowhere else to go. The vast armies of the Erkúns had laid waste to all the realms of the east. Those had not stayed to collaborate with their new rulers, were either dead or homeless. The Erkún's defeat at the River Tiba was cancelled out by their capture of the Bridges of Algas and Asor. Outnumbered and outfought, the surviving multi-racial rabble was forced to take refuge in the dark woodlands of Lake Birthas. Yet, their enemy saw no need to follow them among the trees, at least for now.

Indeed, the Emperor of the Underworld (who personally oversaw the eastern campaign) ordered his vast army to encircle the woodlands, and to prevent any Insect from escaping. After all, why waste energy fighting an exhausted foe, when you can merely let him starve to death?

Lazimóff woke from his slumber at around eight o'clock in the morning. For some months he had no longer been the exuberant, confident sorcerer of three years ago. Indeed, so many moons of conflict had left the Bumble Bee scarred, weary and considerably more cynical. The occasional victory won over the enemy (such as a minor rear-guard action in the Golden Mountains a year earlier), was not enough to keep his hopes up. He had seen far too much misery, suffering and death to be enthused about his side's chances. He was but one Kaldára, facing multiple foes of terrible power. How could he possible turn the tide in the face of so much darkness?

The environment in which he found himself immersed, hardly inspired confidence either. The stench of Insect filth filled his tent, as well as a rather more disturbing odour: that of the Black Leaf. This rare, exotic plant which grew along the eastern banks of the River Anozáth close to the great port city of Ashúr had been used as a powerful narcotic for many centuries via the smoking of pipes. Its consumption left the smoker in a stupor of ecstasy, yet in turn consumed by a terrible addiction which often killed him or her in a matter of months. In light of their terrible predicament, many Insects huddled around Lake Birthas had turned to this eastern poison in order to make their almost inevitable passing, all the more painless.

Despite the misery and cynicism which hung in the air, Lazimóff did his utmost not to be consumed by it, and decided to head to the royal tent that every evening. For the sake of the peoples of Insectdom and their rulers, he had to do his duty, no matter his own personal reservations about their fate. Upon entry into the royal tent he found King Robert of Skrallog (the only surviving monarch of the east) standing over a table covered by a map of the local area.

Around him were several Spider nobles and military officers, as well as a smattering of Snails, Bees, Flies and Maggots of similar social standing. The presence of Flies and Spiders in the same encampment had been problematic to say the least. The destruction of their lands by the Underworld's hordes had left the bitterest of foes with no choice but to co-operate. Nevertheless, outbreaks of violence were frequent and Lazimóff did his utmost to prevent them from escalating. Indeed, even in an elitist gathering such as this, the Kaldára kept the Spiders and the Flies physically apart from each other.

In this tense situation the remnants of Insectdom's old order bickered over the next course of action. The military situation was hopeless. Totally surrounded and outnumbered, the prospect of conventional, open battle with the enemy was looked upon in absolute horror. Even those that could fly were unable to flee, with Erkún circling above and blasting any creature out of the sky. After much argument, it was basically decided that the refugees had but two choices: either remain in the woodland, or breakout. The latter option was supported most fervently by Lazimóff, the Spiders and the Snails and with a great deal of reluctance by the other races present.

As to how this breakout would be carried out, it was decided in the late hours of the evening that a great push forward would be made westwards the following dawn, with the aim of breaking through the encirclement and to flee westwards to the Valley of Leaves (a region rich in the diamond and herb trade, dominated by its inhabitants the Slugs): one of the very few remaining natural safe havens in this part of the world. The first wave would be composed entirely of soldiers, while the rear would be brought up by civilians. There were no illusions about the outcome of this gamble. Casualties would almost certainly be high, and the chances of success were small.

Nevertheless, in the minds of all those present, there was no realistic alternative to the one proposed. The chances of relieved by western forces at this moment in time were minimal, and a lake surrounded by woods was hardly an ideal natural stronghold to bleed a numerically superior enemy to death. With the final decision taken, the multi-racial council of war returned to their respective encampments to inform their underlings of the situation at hand and the action which was to be taken. The reaction was one of grim acceptance and submission. There was not even the slightest hint of opposition, despite the severe risk that it entailed. The attack was to commence at dawn, and that was final. All that remained now was for the wretched Insects to pray to their Gods and to ask for mercy.

It was at the crack of dawn, when the Emperor of the Underworld was awoken from his slumber by one of his underlings. Despite his immediate irritation, he soon realised that it had to be an urgent matter. After all, any wretched creature who dared to wake him on the grounds of something he considered trivial, the punishment could be most severe. This time however, a pressing issue was at hand.

Erkún scouts had located movement from within the woodlands surrounding Lake Birthas. Mobilisation of the troops was therefore of paramount importance. Despite the impending prospect of another battle, Hordar was relatively untroubled by such an eventuality. After all, in his confident mind victory was all but secured. The vast majority of his foes' forces had been routed in many past skirmishes, unable to withstand his mighty hordes.

Yes, there had been the occasional setback such as the defeat at the Bridge of Elubí. Indeed, the Emperor mourned the loss of so many Erkúns and underlings at the banks of the Tiba. Nevertheless, he came to the conclusion that the defeat was perhaps a blessing in disguise. At long last he had sensed the true intentions of the treacherous Akran Súr. He had long suspected his dear friend's ambitions, but never had he thought that the insolent upstart would have had such a clear desire to supplant him. The thought of his dearest childhood friend wishing to betray him, made him sick to his stomach. He would have torn out his throat, if he had the chance.

Therefore, he secretly breathed a sigh of relief at his former friend's death. His authority was now totally unchallenged, and with a few more victories he would go down in history as the Emperor which ruled below and above the Surface of the world, giving land and power to even the most lowly of Erkúns. It would be an empire of based on the recognition of the real nature of Insects, and not on fantasies like those favoured by the pompous Kaldáre vermin. The Insects would live autonomous lives in their realms, with tribute payments and oaths of loyalty to the Erkún masters as the only conditions for existence. Such an entity would surpass even the Empire of the Red Banner, and to last until the end of the earth itself. Oh, what joy it gave Hordar to think of such an eventuality.

"So, the Insect scum have decided to attack us, have they?" asked the Emperor contemptuously.

"Indeed, that seems so, Your Excellency. As pathetic as the rabble is, we must prepare our forces immediately for their imminent attack. An assault on our western flank seems to be the most likely outcome," replied the Southern Clan leader.

"Let it be reinforced, then. I want them stopped in their tracks with haste. Our forces to the west and east are to then advance towards each other, and to clear the woodlands within the next week," ordered Hordar.

"Thy will be done, Sire," said the Southern Clan leader submissively.

Soon, the orders were sent down the countless ranks of the Underworld to prepare for the inevitable assault upon their lines to the west. The prospect of another battle greatly pleased the many thousands of Ants and Wasps, whose thirst for blood still remained as strong as ever despite countless skirmishes. Very soon, they would be able to feast on the remains of those deluded fools who still dared to challenge the might of the Underworld.

Meanwhile, at a distance of no more than an Insect Mile from the Erkún's ranks, stood the shivering and apprehensive rabble of refugees at the western edge of the woods, concealed partially among the trees. The soldiers were deathly quiet, and the civilians were trembling with fear, many of them disorientated due to the effects of the Black Leaf beginning to wear off. Despite the obvious reluctance of the group to move, Lazimóff and Robert knew that they had to lead by example. Therefore, the Kaldára and King Robert stepped forward, with the latter brandishing a large battle axe in one of his powerful limbs and raising it above his head.

"Soldiers and peoples of the free world, hear my words! Before you stand the filthy slaves of darkness! The very beings that have slaughtered countless numbers of our kin! Thousands of noble Insects who preferred to die with honour than to cower before the Erkúns and to live a life of misery and slavery! Now they wish to finish what they started, by feasting on our blood if need be! There is no escape from the truth, my friends! Beyond those wretched ranks of dark underlings, lies our only possible salvation! I will not deny that death is the most probable outcome that awaits us. However, if we are to go to our doom, then let it be on our own terms! I do not ask you to fight for me, or for any other noble King or Queen, or for honour. But in the name of those who fell before us, those who refused to bend the knee to tyrants! For the fallen!" bellowed King Robert defiantly, followed by a booming cheer in response from his troops.

"Now is the hour, free peoples of Insectdom! Fulfil your obligations in the name of all those who you hold most dearly! To the west I say!" cried Lazimóff with equal passion, followed by the blowing of battle horns, from the realms of Thámrod, Skrallog, and Gagorland among others.

Slowly but surely, the great mass of desperate but defiant Insects charged forward across the fields westwards into the path of the hordes of the Underworld. Fearing a terrible onslaught, Lazimóff raised his staff, shooting a bolt of red light into the sky and transforming itself into a gigantic protective dome above the great multitude. Much to his relief, the Erkúns circling above could not penetrate this protective shield with their fires, meaning that the soldiers around him could focus solely on launching their full fury against their terrestrial foes, be it with an axe, sword, spear or bow.

Faced with such a desperate charge, the Ants on the ground formed defensive positions, with long pikes and shields at the front, with archers close behind. Once, the great rabble was within range, the soldiers of the Underworld unleashed two devastating volleys of arrows, and flaming harpoons, all of which bounced harmlessly off the dome. The failure of the onslaught to inflict any kind of damage greatly enraged the Erkún commanders, who in turn ordered their Wasps to take to the skies and charge.

Like waves against a cliff, the free peoples of the east crashed into the wall of Ant steel, breaking through the first ranks with momentum, despite losing a great many Insects to being impaled by pikes. Meanwhile, the Wasps, the Hornets and the Blood Brotherhood descended from above, landing between the multi-racial ranks and inflicting great losses on them with their excellent sword fighting skills, before eventually being subdued. Despite the terrible odds, the great mass of refugees managed to advance almost half an Insect mile and only a few hundred yards from the rear of the Ant ranks. Fearing a successful breakout, Hordar barked at his commanders to re-organise and to attack the column from all sides. Once that order was put into practice, the consequences were devastating.

As a result of this manoeuvre, the lightly defended civilian columns were butchered with ease by the ravenous Wasps, Hornets, Mosquitoes and Erkúns, who incinerated all stood in their path, including the very woodlands in which some refugees had chosen to remain. Within a matter of forty or fifty Insect minutes, more than eighty percent of the civilian ranks had been massacred. The slaughter of so many defenceless Insects would have repulsed many a conventional warrior. Yet, these Underworld creatures were mere killing machines, slaves to the whims of their terrible masters.

As for the soldiers, their predicament was not going much better. While having been able to slay a large number of foes, their own casualties were also beginning to mount, and their advance was stalling at a rapid rate. Were it not for the terrible predicament that these poor souls were in, one could not but wonder at the sight of thousands of Insects of different races, some of whom had been eternal enemies but two years ago, fighting side by side against a common foe.

By late morning, the fate of Lazimóff, Robert and their followers seemed to be all but decided. The ravenous hordes of the

Underworld had managed to slay more than half of their soldiers, and had them totally surrounded, along with the smattering of refugees who had survived and had decided to take up arms with their military brethren. The Kaldára was verging on exhaustion. Despite having slain a number of Erkúns and countless Wasps and Ants, he feared that he could not go on much longer.

However, his hopes were dealt a great blow when his dear friend King Robert was struck down in battle. After having slain many foes, the great Spider was finally felled by an Ant pike through his chest. The sight of his trusted companion drawing his last breath wounded Lazimóff as much as a physical weapon would have done. For the first time ever, he felt so very alone.

Consumed by grief, the headstrong Kaldára was troubled in the midst of battle, by the sound of a dark voice inside his head: the Emperor of the Underworld himself was speaking to him directly. He could feel the Erkún's presence, barely a few hundred meters on his right flank.

"You have failed, Kaldára. Admit your fault and be done with your life. There is nothing left for you here on this earth, only death. You and your order are now devoid of purpose. The age of the Erkún is upon you. The Peace of the Tiba is undone," said Hordar, barely concealing his smug satisfaction.

"When I die, and die I shall, it shall be after having removed your head from shoulders!" replied Lazimóff angrily.

The initial feeling of grief was now replaced by one of uncontrollable rage. Devoid of hope and purpose, in his final moments the Bumble Bee would focus his efforts entirely on one sole objective: to kill the Emperor. No matter the peril, no matter the obstacles, Lazimóff would stop at nothing to get to the wretched Erkún. With consummate ease, the Kaldára swatted Ants and Wasps with the power of his staff, until finally he reached the Emperor, protected by four warriors of the Blood Brotherhood.

After much fierce battle, Lazimóff managed also to slay the terrible fiends which protected their ruler, leaving him face to face with Hordar. The Kaldára blocked bolt after bolt with his staff and managed to get within sword's distance of his foe to land a killer magical blow. Alas, the Erkún also possessed quick reflexes and managed to strike a forceful blow with his right limb which struck the Kaldára squarely in the face and sent him flying more than one hundred Insect metres. The strike had left Lazimóff totally unconscious and unfit for battle. He would play no more part in this fight, left to the mercy of the terrible doom which was upon himself and his brothers in arms.

⸺⸺◆☙◆⸺⸺

Several hours had passed, when Lazimóff finally woke up from his unintended slumber. Slowly, the young Kaldára opened his eyes, squinting at the sky above. He felt a considerable degree of disorientation at first, not entirely sure where he was. Once he managed to get his bearings and at least sit up, he finally perceived the events that had come to pass around him.

What struck him most of all, was how quiet it was. The battle had seemingly ended, with the foul stench of thousands of fallen Insects lying heavily in the air. Indeed, Lazimóff found himself surrounded by mountains of corpses on all sides. A thick fog hanged over the battlefield, greatly hindering his vision. Once upon his feet, the Kaldára gathered his staff and sank into a deep meditation. He could sense other creatures nearby, of a surprising nature at that.

Soon, he saw several beings emerging from the depths of the mist and advancing towards him. The young Bumble Bee could not believe what he saw before his very eyes. Before him stood around a dozen Kaldáre dressed elegantly in their long cloaks and wielding their beautiful staffs, including his predecessor Zorza and his friend Múzlak were at the helm.

"Is this a dream? I cannot fathom what I see before me," said Lazimóff, visibly perplexed.

"Relax, young Lazimóff. What you see before you is no figment of your imagination," replied the old Ladybird calmly.

"Múzlak managed to reach you and solicit your aid?" asked Lazimóff.

"Indeed, he did. Despite our initial reservations and displeasure, the Order thought it best to intervene," responded Zorza, looking over at the Dragonfly at her side.

"I had no other choice. The fate of Insectdom was more important than the preservation of petty traditions," replied Múzlak irritably.

"Do not speak ill of the traditions of our forebears, young Múzlak! It is a miracle that this world has been saved, despite the immense incompetence of you and your colleagues!" barked one of the more senior Kaldáre in the ranks. That particular comment irked the Dragonfly greatly, and only self-control restrained him from striking down the old fool in anger.

"What of the Erkúns and their forces? What has become of them?" asked Lazimóff.

"While you were incapacitated, we managed to take them by surprise with our arrival. Thanks to your gallant efforts, the hordes of the Underworld were already weak when we routed them. We have managed to slay many dark beings and save the survivors of your convoy. Alas, the Emperor and some of his minions have managed to escape. Perhaps to Golrum or Elén," explained Múzlak.

"Indeed, the fact that Hordar has fled is particularly irksome. As irksome as the fact that the Erkúns had managed to deceive us so effectively for so many years. That Ambassador of theirs was far more powerful than we all suspected. So strong was his control of dark magic that he managed to conceal his true intentions even from Kaldáre, leaving us blind to all his scheming. Alas, we're all to blame for this catastrophe which has been unleashed upon the world," said Zorza.

"What is to be done then, wise ones?" asked Lazimóff.

"Our task is simple, young Lazimóff: we must gather our strength and then set off southwards. The tide has finally turned, and now all of Insectdom must be fully liberated from the yoke of the Erkúns. From the west and the east, hundreds of Kaldáre will converge upon the occupied lands and restore the justice that they once held so dearly," said Zorza defiantly.

So, the next dawn the great horde of Kaldáre headed southwards to carry out the impending task at hand. Once the lands had been cleared of Underworld forces, the two Kaldára hosts would meet at Sarandos: the very city in which all this evil was originally concocted. Only there, would Lazimóff, Múzlak and Grizwald re-unite once more. The change of mood in Lazimóff was quite astonishing. After having been consumed by despair, hope was finally rekindled in his heart. At long last, the war had an end in sight, and the beautiful prospect of peace. If the battle of Elubí had demonstrated that the Erkúns could not guarantee their total victory in the war, then the battle of Lake Birthas confirmed that the forces of the Underworld were doomed to lose it.

Chapter 12

The last stand

Winter, arrived once more in Insectdom in the year five thousand two hundred and three. Twelve months is a long time for anyone who is at war, no matter who the victor or the vanquished may be. However, the toils of conflict are considerably less unpleasant for the former rather than the latter. After all, the exhilaration of victory in battle is enough to carry many a creature over the line and to withstand the privations that such ordeals entail.

Indeed, this certainly was the case of the Kaldára and their allies across Insectdom. The successful defence of the northern lands had left the armies of the Underworld all but vanquished. With the Erkún's rout at the battle of Lake Birthas, the Kaldáre's bitter foes had spent the last Insect year being driven back further and further south, even if at a great cost to the Kaldáre and their fellow Insect warriors. By early winter, the huge territorial gains of the armies of the Underworld had been all but lost.

The reaction to the liberation of the realms of Insectdom was mixed in many a city, to say the least. While a great many Snails, Spiders, Butterflies and Maggots and others were delighted at the arrival of their liberators, the expulsion of the Erkúns and their ilk from their villages, towns and cities did not signal an end to the bloodshed. Indeed, the joy of the liberated Insects soon turned to bloodthirsty rage as they turned on those neighbours who had decided to throw in their lot with the hordes of the Underworld.

Across countless cities, the vengeance of the peoples of Thámrod, Moriátin, Skrallog and others was manifest throughout these lands, with hundreds of perceived collaborators meeting grizzly ends at the hands of their enraged brethren, and their mutilated bodies put on display throughout the realms for all to see the punishments laid out for having colluded with the enemy.

It was in the grand old city of Sarandos, that Grizwald, Lazimóff and Múzlak crossed paths once more and saw right before their eyes, the gruesome manifestation of the rage of the liberated Snails. All the main bridges crossing the River Anozáth were adorned with hundreds of Snail heads impaled onto long spikes, some of which were rendered almost unrecognisable due to decomposition, and the frost.

"The mind of an Insect is a wretched thing at times," said Grizwald solemnly, while looking on at the vicious handiwork on display.

"It is merely a crude manifestation of their most basic nature, Grizwald. After all, is not the mind of a Kaldára or an Erkún any worse?" said the ever so cynical Múzlak.

"I do hate it when you are right, Múzlak. Still, one day there will come a time to properly educate these beasts," said Lazimóff.

"A rather grandiose remark, don't you think Grizwald? It seems that we have a Kaldára who seeks to be Emperor, in our midst," replied Múzlak scornfully, while looking over at the Praying Mantis.

"Enough talk, Múzlak! There is only so much cynicism that one can take," responded Grizwald irritably.

"That may be so. However, we must concentrate on the task at hand, my friends. Our war is not yet won, and much remains yet to be done," remarked Lazimóff.

"Indeed, there is. It is not long now before we gather with the rest of our Order on the borders of the Gala Gún," said Grizwald.

"I cannot help but wait for such an eventuality. With a bit of luck, what remains of the Erkún filth will capitulate by dawn," said Múzlak confidently, despite the exhaustion.

"I admire your confidence in the face of adversity, my friend," said Grizwald with a warm smile.

It was almost midnight that very day, when the five dozen or so Kaldáre gathered outside the imposing maze which concealed the Door of the Underworld. With the armies of the Erkúns having been decimated and scattered in the great counter offensive of the last year (the surviving Ants had fled, while the Wasps all died in battle rather than flee or surrender), the sorcerers from the Lost Island had commanded their Insect allies that their help was no longer needed, and they could finally return home and rest, after three very long years of war.

Only the Kaldáre now stood alone to deal with their lifelong adversaries from the realm below the surface. Most were fresh and ready for battle, unlike the three current custodians of Insecstdom, visibly worn out from many months of campaign, as well as the older Kaldára who were plainly ill at ease at having to interrupt their well-earned retirement.

Among such Kaldáre were Báldur, Zorza and Saldrím, now high representatives of the Grand Council. Despite their irritation, they were wise enough to realise that this great misfortune was not the fault of their replacements. Therefore, such discomfort was to be used in turn against the treacherous Erkúns. One by one they would pay dearly for the terrible misfortune which they had inflicted upon the countless souls across the many lands which they had pillaged.

"Consider yourselves lucky that we have come to your aid, my young friends. Had it not been for the extreme gravity of the situation, you would all be paying for this travesty," said Zorza sternly, glancing over at the younger Kaldára by her side. Indeed, neither Grizwald, nor Lazimóff or Múzlak wished to respond to their powerful predecessor, perhaps out of both fear and shame.

"What is done, is done, Zorza. Not even the Gods can alter what has come to pass. All that remains now is to deal with the situation at hand, no matter how unpleasant it may be," interjected Báldur.

"I couldn't have put it better myself, my friend," said Saldrím, visibly pleased with his fellow Kaldára's remarks.

"Alas, you are right, Saldrím. There is now the small issue of getting through this impenetrable maze surrounding the Gala Gún. I sense a dark presence among these rocks. I fear that our path will be perilous," said Zorza warily.

"I would have it no other way," said Lazimóff confidently.

"Oh I do admire the youth for their enthusiasm. It reminds me a great deal of what I once was, when I first set foot on this wretched earth," said Báldur nostalgically.

Nevertheless, there was little time for reminiscing. With all the available Kaldáre now marshalled before the rocky labyrinth. It was now time for them to move in. In order to move more effectively, the magical force was divided into three groups. Zorza would lead a detachment to fly over the maze, joined by Kaldáre such as Múzlak. Meanwhile, the rest of the sorcerers were divided into two other ground forces led by Báldur and Saldrím, who would enter the maze from the east and west respectively, with Grizwald joining the former and Lazimóff the latter.

Quite what they would encounter among these terrible rocks remained a mystery to every Kaldára present. Whatever it was, they expected one final defiant act from their foes.

Slowly but surely, the mighty conjurers made their way either above the maze, or directly through it on foot. Indeed, Grizwald, Lazimóff and some of their fellow sorcerers were visibly apprehensive at having to walk through this imposing labyrinth of razor-sharp rocks, their staffs thrust out in all directions, as if to expect an ambush at any given moment. The almost total silence in the dark, gave the impression that such an underhanded assault, was but a few moments away from being carried out.

After an hour of travel, all the Kaldára parties arrived at the Gala Gún itself safe and sound. Had it not been for their gift of magical foresight, they too would have driven mad in a fruitless chase around the almost impassable maze, in the manner of many mere mortal Insects who had not been blessed with such a power. Such considerations however, were of little importance to the Kaldáre now. There were more pressing issues at hand than their fortune.

Having all successfully reached the door of the Underworld, the sorcerers swiftly encircled it completely. This now meant that any creature that wished to escape, would find a Kaldára in his or her path. But, for now the door remained shut. Whether it would be opened or not, was soon to be discovered.

With the entrance to the final bastion of the Erkúns surrounded from all sides, the elders of the Grand Council strode forth towards the mighty stone with its golden markings. One could expect that such powerful beings such as Kaldáre would be able to open such a door. Yet, this was not the case. For the power of the Erkúns in the Underworld was so strong, that they and only they, could open the gate which they themselves had forged.

Faced with such an impasse, Báldur stepped forth, wielding his long staff and with a deep, booming voice which echoed across the lands, he spoke:

"In the name of the Kaldára Order and the people of Insectdom, I command the lords of the Underworld to come forth! Come forth and face the justice that should be so rightfully done upon them! In the name of the Gods themselves and all that is divine, we swear that that no harm shall be bestowed upon them, should they be willing to surrender. Should they refuse, then they shall suffer the most severe of consequences! The choice is simple, my lords: forgiveness, or death."

Almost a minute of total silence was to pass, before the command of the Kaldára met any kind of response. Exactly one minute after the great Báldur had spoken, the ground began to shake and the circular stone began to transform itself. The rock split open into four separate sections which gradually rose up from the earth and stood up vertically. Fearing some kind of ambush, the Kaldáre fell back to the very edges of the clearing in which the Gala Gún lay.

Suddenly, the loud and distinctive sound of Erkún wings flapping in the wind could be heard rising from the depths of the Underworld. Not before long, did the Kaldáre find Hordar, Emperor of the Underworld, rising himself from the deep and onto the surface, facing the Kaldára Elders. Yet, this was not the mighty monarch which the Kaldáre had seen many a time before.

The albino Erkún was but a broken shadow of his former self. His right, front limb had been lost but a few months earlier at the Battle of Elén and such was his discomfort that he could barely stand upright without falling. His face was scarred beyond all recognition. Indeed, his left eye was also gone, as was his left ear and a portion of his snout. Despite his obvious decrepitude, the Erkún was still a dangerous foe, and was not to be trifled with. With visible discomfort, the once mighty ruler of the Underworld spoke in a snarling tone:

"I would rather suffer eternal punishment at the hands of the most capricious of the Gods, than prostrate myself before you! Over my dead body, will I see my people humiliate themselves before such an unworthy rabble! The time of negotiation is over, Kaldára. Victory or death, are the only options left now. If this is to be our end, then I will make sure that it is worthy of remembrance for generations to come. Your arrogant and condescending species may have the power now, but it will not always be so. Your kind will burn in the fires of doom, in this life or in the next! Of that I am sure!"

"As eloquent as you may be, Sire, your position is hopeless. We outnumber you, and you have no possibility of obtaining final victory. Are you really so proud as to sacrifice what is left of your species, for the sake of your pride?" asked Zorza, visibly confused.

"Better that than kneel before you, whore," growled Hordar.

"Then you leave us no choice. I'm sorry that it has to end in this way," lamented Saldrím.

"Spare me your self-righteousness! I will not have any more of this sanctimonious talk!" barked the Emperor of the Underworld.

"So be it, Sire," replied Báldur, in a stern, almost menacing tone.

With the conversation concluded, the albino Erkún let out a bellowing roar which shook the ground beneath the Kaldáre, followed by a bolt of flame which engulfed a Kaldára to Grizwald's right in a lethal fire. Within a matter of seconds, a furious rabble of half wounded Erkúns and Blood brothers emerged from the Gala Gún and charged towards their foes in one final, futile act of defiance.

The battle itself was brief and bloody. At a minimal cost of just half a dozen of their order, the Kaldáre managed to obliterate the onslaught that fell upon them, in a great shower of light, lightning and flames. For all their rage, the Erkúns no longer had the strength to repel the Kaldáre completely, and as a result all lay dead or dying, along with their wretched slaves. With the final Erkún assault totally broken, the Kaldáre moved forward towards the edge of the door of the Underworld.

Simultaneously, around a dozen of them took upon the task of slaying the Erkún which were not yet dead. Indeed, Hordar himself remained alive, if barely. However, the Emperor of the Underworld was soon put of his misery by Lazimóff, who picked up the sword of a fallen Blood Brother and drove the mighty blade through the neck of the moribund Erkún, until he gave out one last, rattling breath.

"Gather around brothers and sisters! We have now but one more task to complete: we must now cleanse the Underworld itself, of the filth that remains!" barked Saldrím.

Grizwald immediately realised what a terrible order his elder had given. He could not believe that a Kaldára could be capable of such an abomination.

"With all due respect, my Elders, I must protest! The filth, of which you speak, is naught but female Erkúns and their infants! How can you possibly give such an order? Since when do Kaldáre slaughter the defenceless?" cried Grizwald angrily.

"Now is not the time for sentimentality, young Grizwald. Obey the orders given to you," replied Saldrím sternly.

"Indeed, I will not! I have seen much darkness in the past three years. I have seen Insects and Erkúns commit unspeakable acts in the name of their causes. I will not believe that ours is righteous, if we stoop to the level of our foes!" said Grizwald, visibly more agitated with every passing second.

"Griwald, please, control yourself!" interjected Múzlak grabbing his colleague by the shoulder.

"Unhand me, I say! I will have no part in such butchery!" replied Grizwald, pushing the Dragonfly's limb off his shoulder.

"Be silent! Enough of this idealistic buffoonery! The order has been given and it shall be obeyed! Your fellow brothers and sisters of the Order stand in unison. Only you are so blind as not to see the logic. The Erkúns are too dangerous to be kept alive! As long as one single Erkún lives, the threat to the peace of Insectdom will be eternal and it will see nothing but civil war without end!" barked Báldur angrily.

"I do not believe it! I will not believe it! There must be some other way! Why must the innocent perish for the crimes of others?" cried Grizwald.

"Silence!" boomed Zorza, striking the Praying Mantis unconscious with a bolt of red light from her staff.

With the sole opponent now silenced, the remaining Kaldáre turned to their task at hand. In unison, the mighty sorcerers raised their staffs high above their heads.

"Brothers and sisters ignite your staffs!" cried Báldur.

In a flash, the sky above the Gala Gún was illuminated by around fifty bright rays of light shooting up vertically into the heavens.

"Unite!" boomed Saldrím, whose order was met by a joining of the lights into a single, multi-coloured, almost blinding beam which shot down into the depths of the Underworld.

Like an uncontrollable wild fire, this almost divine-looking light spread across all the lands of the Underworld at an incredible speed. All that lay in the path of this wave, perished swiftly. Indeed, as Grizwald slowly awoke from his slumber, the screams of hundreds of female Erkúns and their infants could be heard echoing from the depths below. Such shrieking howls of pain, made the Praying Mantis physically sick, who in turn vomited to his side. It was not until the ceasing of the screams of the wretched creatures, that the Kaldára light was finally extinguished.

White smoke rose from the Gala Gún. An eerie silence now hung over the former Erkún stronghold. The Kaldáre looked over the edge of the mighty stone door, uneasily. Their magical intervention had worked. After all, no life could have withstood such a barrage of magic, and as a result, not a single living creature could be sensed in what remained of the once, mighty and imposing Underworld.

———◆≋◆———

The long walk back to Sarandos through the barren lands was as silent as the night itself. Indeed, not a single Kaldára wished to utter a word to his or her fellow sorcerers. Indeed, many of them were still digesting what had just happened. After three years of unspeakable misery and hardship, the greatest war of their age, was now finally over. The Erkúns: eternal foes of the Kaldáre were no more. At long last, the peoples of Insectdom could enjoy the peace which they had craved for so long. How exactly that peace would take shape, would remain a mystery unknown to all mortals.

It was early morning when Grizwald, Lazimóff and Múzlak rose from their long slumber and moved to one of the large balconies of the royal palace of Sarandos. One week had passed since the end of the war at the Gala Gún. Yet, its aftermath was still taking its toll on those who witnessed it unfold. Grizwald had not uttered a single word since then, and merely looked on numbly at the Snails below who were slowly rebuilding their ruined city.

"One day, you are going to have to speak, Grizwald. You cannot remain silent forever," said Múzlak in a concerned tone.

"Leave him be, Múzlak. It is not our place to comment on how one should react to such ordeals as those that we have experienced," said Lazimóff.

"I have nothing to say, my friends. No words can express the hollowness which I feel in my heart," replied Grizwald solemnly.

"I understand your pain, my friend. However, you must not let your emotions get the better of you. What is done is done. Not even the Gods can alter what has come to pass," said Múzlak.

"Are you not in the least bit ashamed by what we have done? Are you not in the least bit concerned that we have become the very bloodthirsty butchers we fought against?" asked Grizwald.

"It is better not to reflect on such things, Grizwald. I cannot allow myself to be consumed by such thoughts. My capacity to do my duty depends on it," replied Múzlak in an almost exasperated fashion.

"The Dragonfly speaks wise words, my friend. You must put these terrible events behind you as soon as possible. The peoples of Insectdom need us now more than ever. We cannot allow ourselves to falter in our duty," said Lazimóff in a bid to rouse the spirits of his friend.

"I cannot guarantee that such a thing will come to pass, my friends," replied Grizwald gloomily.

"Then there is nothing we can do for you, my friend," said Múzlak with an equally pessimistic tone.

———◆☙◆———

With the world now at peace and its races gradually resuming their natural ways of life, the large cohort of Kaldáre which had come to their aid, was now departing and heading northwards to return to the land from whence it came. Most left with a strong sense of self-satisfaction and indeed relief, at the work they had done on this earth. Others, such as the eldest of the sorcerers, felt nought but exasperation at having to come to the aid of such a wretched place, and yearned for a swift return to the shores of the Lost Island and its pearl-white beaches.

As for the three Kaldáre whose duty it was to watch over Insectdom, their paths were to separate once more. Indeed, they bode each other a warm farewell in the spring of that year on the banks of the River Tiba. Henceforth, they would now only communicate via meditation, lest a new and terrible crisis engulf the world once more.

Having been spared punishment by the Grand Council on the Lost Island for having returned before time, Múzlak headed southwards. It had been decided that the young Dragonfly was to patrol the lands south of the River Tiba, and to watch over the Gala

Gún until the end of his time on Insectdom (in order to guarantee that no living creature could open the door of the Underworld once more). He was to remain in contact with the races in these lands, giving his counsel whenever possible.

As for Lazimóff, his mission was to roam the lands of the east, never settling in one place for more than a few months. Here that the mighty Bumble Bee would continue to expand his power and his wisdom, in the wildest parts of the world, many of which would remain disputed between multiple races for centuries to come.

Last but not least, was Grizwald. After having endured a humiliating tongue lashing from the Grand Council, the Praying Mantis reluctantly agreed to carry out his duties in the west, with a semi-permanent residence in Nalgála. From here he would set forth to then travel to the most distant corners of these lands and settle whatever dispute that could arise.

The years would pass, and still he would be plagued by the immense guilt which he felt. For a long time after the Great War the Kaldára continued to suffer nightmares, remembering vividly the terrible massacre which he witnessed at the foot of the Gala Gún. Nevertheless, his only consolation was that slowly but surely, as months became years and years became decades, the screams which had troubled his sleep for so long, finally died out.

THE END

Printed in the United States
By Bookmasters